THE BLACK LEGION

THE Black Legion

William Vaughan

y Lolfa

First impression: 2008

© William Vaughan & Y Lolfa Cyf., 2008

Cover design: David Wenzel

ISBN: 9781847710772

Printed on acid-free and partly recycled paper
and published and bound in Wales by
Y Lolfa Cyf., Talybont, Ceredigion SY24 5AP
e-mail ylolfa@ylolfa.com
website www.ylolfa.com
tel 01970 832 304
fax 832 782

ONE

MISS MEGAN

In the autumn of 1796, in a forgotten corner of West Wales, it was hard to believe that the drums of war were echoing across Europe. Hundreds of miles away, the French king's head had been sliced off and countless working men were butchered every day. But, in the port of Fishguard, the townsfolk still put to sea to fish or carry coal. They knew little of the outside world, nor cared much for it.

In this backwater, Thomas Phillips, a bright fifteen year old, lived with his widowed mother.

One soft September morning, she said to him, 'You're a good lad, Tom, and I'm proud of you, but it's time you found some employment. Major Meredith wants you as his manservant. He thinks you've more about you than the other town-boys and has offered to provide your food, lodging and a wage of sixpence a day.

'Pentower is a Christian house and the Major's promised to teach you to read the Scriptures as well as your household duties. He'll keep you busy, but you've never been afraid of hard work. And you'll be allowed to walk home on the Lord's Day so that we can go to chapel together. It's a generous offer, son.'

'I'd love to be able to read our family Bible, Mam, but I should miss you too much to be able to study. And you'd be lonely on your own. I would rather stay here!' Tom protested.

'Bless you, dear, you won't be leaving me for ever,' his mother replied. 'If you take a short-cut through the fields, you can walk home inside an hour. And the Major doesn't use the whip nor lash! At Pentower, you'll have the sun, the open air and the fields about you. Being surrounded by such beauty and living decently is just the work for a Christian lad.'

Tom was silent for a moment. He gazed into the fire which always burnt in the kitchen grate. 'You're right, Mam,' he sighed. 'What more could I want?'

'Major Meredith has promised to call upon us for tea at five o'clock. You can pack a bag and return with him to begin your new life,' his mother continued, a little wistfully in spite of her bravado.

It was almost six when Major Owen Meredith arrived, accompanied by his daughter, the only child of the richest farmer in the neighbourhood and reputed to be one of the most elegant young women in the county of Pembrokeshire.

'I'm sorry we're late,' the tall man apologised. 'Megan wanted to visit the milliner's.'

The maiden blushed, but said nothing. She was staring into the youth's deep brown eyes. He was attractive, especially his golden hair and olive-tinted skin. Unnerved by her admiring gaze, Tom glanced at the flagstone floor.

Miss Megan took off her new bonnet and held its sky-blue ribbons so that it hung in front of her. When she walked, her skirt moved enough to show off her shoes, with their silver buckles. Her ears peeped out from the ringlets of jet-black hair which cascaded down each side of her narrow head. Her teeth shone and she smelt of rose petals. Tom had never seen such beauty in all his life.

Without waiting for any formal introduction, Miss Megan crossed the room and shook his hand. She did not realise that the mere touch of her silky skin caused his heart to skip and his knees to tremble.

'I know who you are,' she said, laughing playfully. 'My father has been speaking of you all day. He tells me you're to come to live with us.'

'Megan!' her father exclaimed. 'Whatever can Mistress Phillips think of a girl who doesn't wait to be introduced but goes right up to her son and begins to talk so familiarly?'

Tom's mother chuckled and said, 'Well, I don't suppose it displeases him.'

Tea, using the best crockery and a linen table-cloth, was soon over. At his mother's command, Tom went to the corner of the room where a wooden chest stood and removed his square coat and tricorn hat. He rubbed them briskly with a horse-hair brush and fastened the buttons.

After bidding their farewells, Megan and her father, arm-in-arm, strolled out into the evening air towards their carriage. Shadows stretched in the late sunlight. Tom and his mother exchanged hugs and kisses as they followed. Then the youth clambered onto the landau's front wheel and levered himself alongside the coachman. The harness rattled and the horses' hooves rang as they trotted out of Fishguard. In spite of the fine weather, both of the retractable hoods were raised so that Tom was unable to hear the praise which Miss Megan was already according him.

The carriage clattered over the crest of a hill and Tom saw the sprawling farmhouse which stood close to a mysterious round tower set in an orchard of apple trees. In the darkening landscape, Pentower seemed strangely sinister. The youth realised that he was about to enter a different world, and it was a daunting prospect.

The coachman tried to lift his passenger's spirits by saying, 'For a daughter like Miss Megan, I'd sacrifice everything I have. She's a lovely lass and no mistake.'

'There's no doubt about that, sir,' Tom agreed.

The plump man grinned. 'You don't call me "sir"! My name's Dai – Dai Williams. As soon as we halt, jump down and open the door for the Master, there's a good lad.'

Tom did as he was told and, after the Major took Megan's head in his hands to kiss her brow and wish her goodnight, was granted a smile to melt his heart.

'Dai, take young Thomas and show him to his room. He's to share with James Bowen in the attic, but he can help with the horses first. As night is drawing in, you can attend to the shutters and doors too. See that he gets some food in his belly before you retire.'

The newcomer sat at a long table in the high-ceilinged, copper-lined kitchen. He was chewing a chunk of bread topped by a sliver of cheese when someone said, 'What have we here? That'd better not be my supper you're eating.'

The voice had come from the doorway where a middle-sized, slender man stood. Although he could not have been much above thirty years of age, his thick tawny hair was already streaked with silver. His eyes seemed to be constantly searching for something and his body would not remain quiet for a second. He had the air of an uneasy soul.

Tom coughed nervously and said, 'Dai gave me this.'

The man grunted. 'Then you won't mind if I have some of it, will you?' And without further ado, he helped himself to what was left of the supper. 'I've been sweating at the forge all day, tempering scythes. My need of it is greater than yours.'

He smirked as he poked his finger into Tom's shoulder.

'What do they call you?' he demanded.

'Thomas Phillips,' came the curt reply.

'Well, boyo, you do as you're told and keep your trap shut. That way, we'll get on just fine.'

After a few hours of troubled sleep in which his mother loomed large, Tom woke with a start and a shiver. The garret was bathed in moonlight. He looked across at the mattress where Bowen had been snoring earlier, but his room-mate had disappeared into the night.

He yawned and tried to sleep again, but failed. As he tossed and turned, his thoughts drifted to his father, a timber merchant, who had died when he was only seven. He recalled how he would sit on his father's lap, put his mouth close to his ear and whisper into it. Then he would throw his arms around that strong neck and they would clasp each other close. Tom had not wept in a long time, but when he recalled the dreadful day when his father had set sail for Liverpool – never to return – sad, salty tears stung his eyes. He lay and waited for the sunrise to bring some welcome light into his suddenly lonely world.

TWO

THE FORGE

A line of grey smoke rose from a stubby chimney and clambered into the cloudless sky. Making scythes for harvesting was hot work in the coldest of months but, on a sparkling September afternoon, the forge was an inferno. Tom, who was deputising for the absent James Bowen by working the leather bellows, had to brush beads of sweat from his forehead and chest.

'Give us a song, lad!' the blacksmith shouted.

Tom hesitated, and then began to sing in an unsteady baritone:

What care we for others' pain,
That pass their lives in sorrow?
Give to us but sun and rain
And thoughts not of the morrow!

His voice mixed with the hammering on the anvil to create a merry noise.

Major Meredith, out for a walk with his daughter, looked at the smoke, heard the clanging and singing, and wondered what was going on. As the couple drew closer, they could hear the song's lyrics. The Master removed his hat, entered and smiled when he saw the youth hard at work.

Miss Megan stood at the threshold, fascinated by the newcomer's lean, damp torso which was glinting in the forge's glare. Her cheeks flushed. She had never been so affected by the sight of a half-naked body before. Only with considerable reluctance did she tear her eyes from Tom's taut stomach muscles to watch the blacksmith place a rod of iron into the fire with a pair of long-handled tongs. Then he drew it out, spitting its burning fragments everywhere, and began beating it again, clearing away the dross which clung to the red-hot metal.

Eventually, the blacksmith stopped working and glanced up. He smiled and wiped his powerful paw before offering it to his superior. The Major grasped it with a hold that would have made a weaker man flinch.

'It's a pleasure to bid a stranger welcome,' the blacksmith laughed.

Major Meredith turned back his shirt sleeves to the elbows and grabbed the hammer with both hands. He swung it through the air and over his shoulder, bringing it down upon the iron with force and precision. Up and down it went. A dozen times, his blows made the anvil tremble. Then the blacksmith gave him a sign to stop. The Major let the hammer glide through his hands onto the earth floor. He took out a handkerchief and wiped his forehead. He sucked in a deep breath, puffed out his cheeks and smiled with satisfaction.

'Well, lad,' he said, 'we've got to make up for lost

time with you. There's nothing pulls a fellow back so much as not being able to read and write. If a man's ignorant, he can't read his Bible and know the difference between right and wrong. It's all too easy for such men to spend their lives in crime. Flogging and hanging aren't the answer. What they need is somebody to show them the beauty of learning and how to lead a Christian life.'

He paused and then asked, 'How did you sleep? In this devilish heat, you'll need a strong constitution.'

'I slept well enough, sir,' Tom replied, less than honestly. 'And I'll be of service to you and Miss Megan in whatever ways I can. My Mam would expect nothing less.'

The Major nodded in approval and gave his servant a slap on the back, an action much envied by his daughter, who had already noticed the golden hair which trailed in an inverted triangle from the nape of Tom's neck down the top notches of his spine. She would have relished the chance to touch his skin which, otherwise, was smooth as marble.

Her father was silent for a moment, frowned and then added, 'I hope I shall be more successful with you, my boy, than I've been with James Bowen. I feared he was going to the bad. I tried everything but all to no purpose; there was no making head nor tail of him.

'When John Mortimer dismissed him from Trehowel farm, I thought he'd be grateful for a second chance but it seems I was wrong...'

'It's a pity his father never taught him a handicraft,'

the blacksmith interrupted. 'But Jim never would listen to advice. Still, perhaps he's not as bad as he's painted.'

'I wish to God that were true!' the Major exclaimed. 'The Devil won't go where he's not invited. The fact is that Bowen was arrested early this morning for stealing horses. He will be face-to-face with the magistrates in Haverfordwest soon enough.'

The blacksmith sighed through his ragged beard.

But Megan asked hopefully, 'Will he be sent out to the convict settlements in Australia with the robbers and murderers?' She had always disliked the lascivious looks which Bowen directed at her and would be pleased to see no more of him, a wish which – unbeknown to her – Tom shared.

'Oh, there's little doubt of that,' the Major answered. 'But remember, my dear, that God loves everybody, even those who do wrong. Now, where are those knives that have got to be hammered? Out with them! We are talking about others being idle and we're no better ourselves.'

In a moment, the blacksmith had drawn a flat piece of iron out of the forge and laid it on the anvil. He nodded and the Master raised the hammer into the air. Down it crashed, time after time. A sense of failure fuelled each mighty blow.

THREE

NOT A NIGHT TO BE BORN

The Indian summer gave way to a stormier October than anyone at Pentower could remember. The kitchen, the warmest room in the farmhouse, became a cosy haven as the days shortened. Tom was not alone in spending more of his time there.

Rain lashed at the windows one afternoon when Dai, his sodden coachman's cloak scattering tiny puddles across the flagstones, stomped in and said, 'Ah, Tom, just the lad I hoped to find. You've a rare skill with animals and I've a mare in foal, even though it's so late in the year. She's near term and I'll be spending the night in the stables. Can I call upon your help?'

Tom nodded. 'I think I could lend a hand.'

The door creaked open a second time and Megan entered. 'How chilled you look, Dai.'

'I hate the cold and wet, Miss.'

'Did I hear you say there will be a foaling tonight?'

'I can't be sure. It depends on the mare. But we

might have to go at any time.'

Megan paused while the clock in the hall chimed three times. 'Then I should like to come with you.'

'The stable is no place for your fine clothes, Miss!' Dai objected. 'You'll be splashed with all sorts of filth and gore.'

But his mistress shook her head and insisted, 'I wish to be present.'

She turned to Tom, laughed and added, 'As we are of similar stature, I shall borrow a shirt and some of your breeches. If I tie back my hair, I think I'll make a serviceable groom! Be good enough to summon me in time.'

A gale was shrieking and the autumn leaves were whirling in the wind as Tom, holding a flickering lantern in one hand, thumped upon Miss Megan's bedchamber door with the other. When she unlocked it, she was clad only in a cotton nightgown which, though loose-fitting, was almost sheer. Tom gazed at her slender, shapely form longer than was commensurate with decorum. At length, he lifted his wide eyes to hers and blurted out, 'Dai says the mare's waxed up which means the foal's on its way, Miss!'

Megan shivered. 'It's not a night to be born, but I'll be with you shortly.'

True to her word, when she reappeared, Megan could have been taken for the sweetest, raven-haired lad in the county. She stood in the doorway, and Tom bowed instinctively. In return, she gave him a quick, intimate smile which made his heart quake.

'Let us go, before she is delivered,' Megan said, while she draped a woollen cloak around her shoulders. There were still spits of rain in the swirling wind as they hurried to the stable. The gale was tugging at the roof and the other horses, unsettled by the weather and the brood mare, were restless. Tom made some clicking noises with his tongue in an attempt to calm them, and he stopped to stroke the white blaze of a favourite gelding.

Though she was not a maiden, there was fright in the mare's eyes. She was sweating, her ears were back and she was stamping and swishing her tail. Her actions were of obvious concern to Megan whose face wore a rare frown.

Dai tried to reassure her. 'Don't you worry, Miss. She knows what she's doing. She's getting the foal into position for the birth. If needs be, she'll even kick herself in the stomach! This one's so big and tardy, I'm sure it must be a colt but, provided he comes head-first, we should have no trouble.' He replied patiently, and with good humour, to all of his mistress's many questions.

As her contractions deepened, the mare lay on her side. Her waters broke and fluid gushed onto the straw bedding. When Tom saw Megan turn her head and grimace, he could not help but laugh out loud.

She blushed with embarrassment. 'I must confess, I wasn't expecting such an effusion, Tom... but I do not poke fun at your lack of knowlege in grammar.'

Suitably chastened, Tom returned his attention to the horse. After a few more vigorous pushes, a bluish-white bag emerged and the foal's forefeet became visible. The mare pressed again and again, but there was no sign of further forward movement so Dai took hold of the forelegs above the fetlock joint and, as she pushed, he pulled.

The membrane-covered head emerged. Dai pulled the sticky coating clear of the foal's nostrils and mouth and then stood back to admire his handiwork. 'She can take care of the rest herself,' he grunted. Moments later, in a bloody mess, the colt slithered into the world.

When the mare was back on her feet, she began licking the foal clean. The colt struggled onto its skinny, wobbly legs and started to suckle its first milk.

Megan stared at the scene and was obliged to brush away a tear. Dai noticed that she was trembling. Not sure whether it was with emotion or the cold, he said, 'If you'll take my advice, Miss, you'll go to bed now. I'll stay here to deal with the after-birth. Kindly escort Miss Megan to her room, Tom. And then get some rest yourself. You look done in, lad.'

The wind had eased and the rain had stopped when the youngsters stepped out into the muddy courtyard together.

A smile swept across Megan's face and she said, 'Jenny, my chambermaid, will wash and return your clothes. They've served me well... as has their owner. You've a way with horses, Tom. A very good way.'

It flitted through his mind that he would prefer to wear the clothes unwashed, with her sweat and scent still upon them, but he kept this notion to himself and merely said, 'Thank you kindly, Miss. Maybe it wasn't such a bad night to be born, after all.'

FOUR

THE NEW YEAR'S BALL

Lady Milford stood beside her husband, the Lord Lieutenant of Pembrokeshire, to welcome the nobility and gentry of the county to their New Year's Ball. She smiled graciously as the guests arrived at the Assembly Rooms in Haverfordwest for the highlight of the winter's entertainment.

Outside, carriages and a few old-fashioned sedan chairs filled the streets. Inside, a great fire warmed the ballroom, the strains of a minuet filled the air and expensive candles lit the shimmering scene.

Lord Milford, resplendent in a navy tailcoat and silk cravat, extended his hand and declared, 'Upon my word, it's Major Meredith and his daughter! It is a pleasure to see you in society again, sir, a great pleasure. The loss of your wife was a grievous blow to us all.'

When Lady Milford offered her gloved hand, the Major touched it with cold fingers.

'This is my daughter, Megan, my lady,' he announced proudly.

'I'm pleased to make your acquaintance, my dear.

That gown is most becoming – muslin, is it not? And such a delightful smile! You're quite the belle of the ball. You must see to it, Major, that your daughter enjoys herself.'

Major Meredith was aware of a note of condescension in Lady Milford's voice, but he was touched by the kindness of the Lord Lieutenant's reception.

'She does not need any encouragement on that score, ma'am.'

Megan took her father's arm and they crossed the room towards a table heaped with food. As they passed, they nodded amiably at the dowagers seated on the plush benches.

When the major-domo announced, in a sonorous voice, the arrival of Lieutenant-Colonel Thomas Knox, all eyes turned to a tall man in his late twenties. Very striking in a scarlet uniform edged with gold braid, he sauntered into the ballroom. Most of the ladies present thought it would be agreeable to dance with such a gentleman.

Colonel Knox glanced around the shining, colourful room. A young lady, who had a natural beauty which required no powder in her hair nor rouge on her cheeks, took his fancy. She wore a high-waisted dress of the lightest green with a lace frill around her pale bosom. A simple gold chain dangled at her throat which made her look like a porcelain figure.

To the accompaniment of violins, bass viols and flutes, the Colonel wandered round the room, bowing at several ladies, but there was only one he considered worth the effort of flirtation.

'And what do they call you, Miss?' he asked Megan, rather too directly.

Nevertheless, she curtsied politely and answered, 'My father named me Megan Meredith, sir.'

'Ah, from Pentower, eh? Well, I am delighted to meet you. And would you do me the honour of the next dance?'

'It would be my pleasure, sir.'

While Megan danced a polonaise with the dashing Colonel, Tom shivered and rubbed his icy hands together. He stared desolately into the warmth and light of the ballroom and realised just how deep was the chasm which separated a servant from his mistress. In his role as a groom, he felt like an outsider, almost an outlaw.

Then Dai told him to brush out the landau and Tom discovered Miss Megan's fan lying on the floor. Gratefully, he grasped the opportunity to return it. He was decently clad but, when he saw the tailcoats, cravats, striped waistcoats and ruffles on display, he wished he wore a finer costume. At the sight of Megan dancing with an imperious-looking officer, he knew that the goddesses of Fate had lured him into an impossible love. But there was nothing he could do other than accept it. He was bewitched.

As soon as the stately music ended, he drew closer to the couple and overheard his mistress ask, 'Is it true the French have invaded Ireland, Colonel? Rumours abound that fifty ships sailed into Bantry Bay before Christmas.'

'Oh, there's no need to worry your pretty head about such matters, Miss Meredith! A fleet, somewhat smaller than you suggest, did reach the Irish shores but, though there was only a small troop of Yeomanry to oppose them, the French lacked the courage to land their forces. And the recent storms have swept most of their ships into the Atlantic Ocean. Providence has destroyed the French fleet as surely it did, in former times, the Spanish armada.'

Though she listened to his every word, Megan gave the appearance of indifference. She was irritated by the Colonel's arrogant and self-opinionated manner, and began to look for some means of escape from his company.

When she noticed Tom heading in her direction, she could not hide her delight. Her eyes shone as he bowed and said, 'You left your fan in the carriage, Miss.'

'Thank you, sir,' she replied, laughing lightly. 'I think your chivalry merits some reward. Would you do me the honour of the next dance?'

Pink roses bloomed in Tom's cheeks as he protested, 'But I don't have the steps, Miss! The country dance is the only one I know.'

'Then that shall be yours,' she declared.

When the fiddlers in the gallery struck up, Megan beckoned to her doe-eyed admirer but, as she was about to slip her hand into his, Colonel Knox intervened, 'May I have this dance, Miss Meredith?'

Megan glanced at Tom and said, 'No, sir, I am already promised to this young gentleman.'

'I do not see any *gentleman*!' Colonel Knox

remarked, in as offensive a tone as he could muster. Before he stalked off to find another partner, he added, 'I only see a servant who has got above his station.'

Tom flinched from such callousness. 'Shall I withdraw, Miss?'

'Indeed, you will not! The Colonel is a haughty and ambitious man, and that's dangerous,' she replied. 'He only commands the Fishguard Fencibles because his father raised the regiment, at his own expense.

'But he told me the Frenchies have abandoned their attack upon Ireland and that we can all sleep safely in our beds tonight. So let us dance!'

When their exertions came to a close, Tom offered Megan his arm and conducted her back to the Major. He wanted to draw her close and kiss her lovely lips. Instead, he bowed to his Master and, with a broad grin on his face, slipped out of the ballroom.

The coachman cracked his whip and a pair of snorting horses began to pull the landau uphill towards the inn where the Merediths were to spend what remained of the night.

Tom's breath smoked in the frosty air as he confided, 'I'll remember this ball for the rest of my life, Dai. I've never felt so happy and hopeful. Earlier this evening, I was so low in spirits that I could've hanged myself. And then I found that fan… '

FIVE

CONVICT SHIP

His Majesty's Ship *Glory* was on course for Botany Bay, with a cargo of convicts. Australia – where Britain dumped its human outcasts – lay 12,000 miles away.

A stiff February breeze kept the English ensign afloat and chilled the convicts who were scattered in groups around huge earthenware pots from which they grabbed food as best they could. Only the officers and soldiers on guard duty were permitted plates, knives and forks. Though they were not many days out of Bristol, several of the convicts had already lost teeth from blows received from the red-coated soldiers. A foul stench pervaded the ship and it was clear that whatever humanity they possessed would soon be beaten out of them.

James Bowen put his hand into one of the dirty pots and pulled out a dead rat! It was nearly as large as the ship's cat and still covered in its skin and fur. Next to him stood a skinny youth. Bowen tore off a leg and pushed it into his face. 'Here, boyo, shove this into your belly. You look in need of it!'

The youngster stared at the sliver of rat, raised his eyes in disgust and shook his head. But Bowen gave a grim laugh, grabbed the lad's head and twisted it towards the torn flesh. He only stopped when one of the soldiers turned round and shouted, 'Don't you know it's forbidden to laugh?'

At once, the third lieutenant came hurrying along the deck and demanded, 'Who's laughing on board?'

'Bowen, sir,' the guard replied.

'Clout him over the shoulders then, to teach him a lesson,' the officer ordered.

The soldier approached Bowen and, catching hold of the club-end of his musket, raised it with both hands and brought it crashing down across the Welshman's shoulders. The youngster cried out, but Bowen did not utter a sound.

The soldier stood still as if waiting for further orders but the officer made a sign as if to say it was enough and he moved off. Shouldering the gun, the soldier continued his rounds.

The ashen-faced youth broke down and began sobbing aloud. Bowen stared at him and said, 'It's no use blubbering, boyo. You must get used to it, and the sooner the better. Look out for those pretty white chewers of yours. Pulling teeth is one of the officers' favourite sports aboard His Majesty's convict ships.'

'But that ain't nothin',' went on a gnarled veteran who had spent years at sea. 'There are worse punishments than that. Bein' tied to a chair so that you can't move yer arms an' legs for days is a sight worse than havin' yer teeth drawn. And many a man don't survive a floggin', when the flesh is torn from his back and his innards are left hangin' out!'

At this appalling news, the youth began to cry even

louder and attracted the attention of the same surly officer who frowned and then squirted some tobacco juice between his teeth onto the deck.

'What the hell are you wailing about?' he snapped. 'It wasn't you who was punished! If you can't shut your row, we can give you some medicine to stop that blasted noise!'

But the downy-chinned lad could not stop himself. The officer leered at James Bowen and ordered, 'Give that son of a bitch a good beating! Give it to him strong and I'll rub the salt in myself.'

The youth turned his eyes towards the sky in desperation and Bowen hesitated. He looked at the officer, waiting for the terrified youngster's release. But the third lieutenant remained cold as stone, expecting his command to be carried out.

'Well, what are you waiting for? Didn't I tell you to let him have it stiff? Hurry up, or I'll have you both tied to the mast for a week!'

Bowen glared at the officer, a ray of hatred gleaming from his eyes. Then he spat onto the deck and declared, 'Is that what you call England's justice? Sending boys to the convict settlements?'

Droplets of sweat stood out on the ruddy-faced officer's brow but, before he could act upon his threats, a weird whistling noise rent the air.

'Dear God, that's cannon-fire!' the officer cried.

As others stooped, he looked out over the bowsprit and bellowed, 'There are four French warships ahead! Guard, summon the Captain at once. Quickly! One broadside and we're all dead men.'

The Captain of the lightly-armed *Glory* knew there was no escape. He accepted his fate and surrendered without a struggle. Any of the enemy frigates' eighteen-pounder guns could have blown his ship to kingdom come. Resistance would have been folly.

When the French longboats arrived, the Captain and his crew were disarmed, put into chains and deposited in the hold of the lugger *Vautour*. The able-bodied convicts were taken aboard the frigate *Vengeance* which was flying Russian colours in a futile attempt to disguise her true origins. Even more surprising was the fact that some of the French troops were wearing scruffy, brownish-black uniforms rather than blue ones.

'Those are British buttons,' Bowen muttered. 'The Frogs have stolen our jackets and dyed them so badly that they're covered in red patches.'

'They look more like a band of ruffians and footpads than soldiers,' the bewildered youth whispered. 'I've never seen such a motley crew.'

'Shut yer gob!' a young officer shouted, in a broad Irish brogue. 'Yez English only speak when you're spoken to.'

'And what about the Welsh?' Bowen retorted, loudly enough to ensure he was heard.

'So you're a Welshman, are yez?' asked the officer, in a much softer tone of voice. 'Come with me. General Tate will want to meet yez.'

To his astonishment, Bowen was marched before an elderly, grizzle-haired man who spoke in a mongrel Irish-American accent. Though some of the junior officers were speaking in French, this invasion force

– if that was its purpose – seemed to be commanded by Irishmen! Bowen could hardly believe his ears and eyes.

'What's your name and where are you from?' the General asked.

'I'm James Bowen from Fishguard, sir.'

'So you know Pembrokeshire and its inhabitants well, then?'

'Aye, sir, I've lived there all my life.'

'And, as a Welshman, I assume you've no fondness for the English, eh?'

Bowen answered truthfully, 'None at all, sir, especially since an English judge told me I was born with vice in my heart and past all cure and that the country was well rid of me. Then he sentenced me to be deported to the other side of the world for stealing a couple of nags.'

The General was old but so tall that the cabin's low roof made him bow his head. He raised his bushy eyebrows and smiled. 'I can't get hold of some of your Welsh names, much less your language, so you're too good a man to be wasted, Mister Bowen, whatever crimes you've committed.

'We've no quarrel with the Welsh people. The English are our enemies. They've treated my countrymen, and yours, cruelly in the past. Now it's time for revenge. Be of service to me and to France and I'll see to it that your future won't be wasted in some penal colony. Your knowledge of the locality will be useful. And you'll be well rewarded for it.'

'Then I'm with you, sir,' Bowen declared. 'Heart and soul!'

'Capital! And do you enjoy a fireworks display?' the General asked.

Puzzled by such an odd question, Bowen merely nodded.

'Well, let's go on deck and you can watch as we turn that foul convict ship into driftwood. We've left some gunpowder aboard and she's alight already. Any minute now, she'll be going up.'

As they emerged into a fresh sea-breeze, the fire reached the powder-barrel. There was a glare, then a thunderous roar and the air was full of smoke and the smell of spent powder. Pieces of timber slapped the waves round about them. James Bowen grinned as the *Glory*, with a strange hissing sound, slid into the depths of the Bristol Channel.

SIX

INVASION

On a bright Wednesday morning in late February 1797, the small French fleet, now flying British colours, sailed into sight of the Pembrokeshire coast. A rare smile of satisfaction crossed James Bowen's face. He cracked his knuckles with the palm and fingers of his left hand as he stared at the homeland he had never expected to see again.

General Tate approached him and said, 'This must seem like a dream to you, eh, Mister Bowen?'

'Aye, sir, it does. I was just remembering the days when I was a lad and used to roam over them hills.'

'Ah, though I spent many years in South Carolina, it's the Ireland of my youth that I recall most fondly,' the veteran sighed in agreement.

'But why do you believe the word of a convict like me?' Bowen asked, genuinely puzzled.

'Men aren't born evil,' Tate replied. 'They become criminals because they've never known and been taught anything else. Soon, a better life will exist for you and your countrymen.

'Though we've only come to Cardigan Bay because the tides and contrary winds made an attack upon Bristol impossible, we have great things to do here. We shall set your people free from slavery to the English! Mark my words, we'll be greeted as liberators. And you, Mister Bowen, will be a hero!

'Stay close to me when we disembark. Your knowledge of the local byways will be invaluable now that we've lost the advantage of surprise. We were spotted by an English cutter off St. David's Head earlier this morning. She was too shallow and too swift for us to follow, but her captain will almost certainly have raised the alarm so we must strike before the iron cools.

'You'll be standing on Welsh soil again before sunset, Mister Bowen. I can promise you that.'

A brisk breeze filled the canvas sails and the *Vengeance* moved steadily on. Bowen had been released from all duties and watched the crew scrubbing decks, splicing ropes, mending uniforms and cleaning muskets.

He stood aside and watched in astonishment when the ship's commander, Commodore Jean Joseph Castagnier, ordered that the hatches be opened.

Up from the holds came a filthy, starving horde of men, most of whom had been convicts forced into service. They had been kept in chains alongside the British captives and a few still wore their wrist and ankle-irons. The decks were soon crammed with a mass of untrained, undisciplined men whose unwashed bodies reeked like rotten fish. The *Legion Noire*, the bulk of the invasion force, was black in heart as well as body.

Suddenly, cries of alarm ran around the ship. A sloop was sailing straight for them! Castagnier realised that this was a cargo ship bound for Fishguard and no threat. He commanded the gunners to fire a warning shot. One blast across her bows was enough to bring the sloop to a halt.

A longboat was again despatched and the master of the *Britannia* was soon standing before his French captors. Castagnier spoke to him respectfully, in excellent English, and even proffered a glass of brandy when the Captain's face blanched at the sight of his vessel being looted. Seagulls shrieked as the sloop was scuttled and slipped into a watery grave, accompanied by roars of approval from the packed ranks of felons. A few bubbles briefly marked the spot where the ship was to lie.

Bowen began to wonder what this unkempt rabble might do once they were free to ravage and plunder. General Tate was a gentleman but he doubted his ability to control these ruffians once they were ashore.

Later that afternoon, Enseigne de Vaisseau Chosel steered the fourteen gun *Vautour* around Pen Anglas Head into the broad waters of Fishguard harbour. The inexperienced commander was shocked to be greeted by a roar of cannon-fire! Alarmed to discover that Fishguard Fort was armed and ready to defend itself, the Enseigne ordered the lugger to beat a swift retreat. He did not know the shot had been a blank and that there were just three rounds of live ammunition in the armoury. He tacked about, returned to the *Vengeance* and sent a message that a direct assault upon the town would be costly.

'Then, sir, shall we moor off Carreg Wastad Point?' Castagnier asked General Tate. 'The cliffs are steep but we should be able to land our men and artillery safely.' What the captain really wanted was to sweep this stinking riff-raff from his ship as quickly as possible.

'*Oui, mon Commodore,* we must put ashore without delay. I shall make my headquarters at Trehowel. Mister Bowen tells me that it's only a mile away and eminently suitable for our purpose. He'll be one of the first ashore. He can lead young Barry St Leger and a band of grenadiers to the farmhouse so that it's ready for me by morning.

'Now, sir, strike that English ensign! And raise the tricolour of France!'

SEVEN

RAISE THE ALARM!

'How old are you now, Tom?' Major Meredith asked.

'I was sixteen last November, sir.'

'And how long have you been with us?'

'Nearly six months.'

'Is that all? You're so much taller and broader that I thought it must be longer. You've learnt a good deal about planting and handling the animals, not to mention your work at the forge and here in the house. What's more important, your reading and writing have improved no end. Your mother must be very proud.'

Tom blushed as he replied, 'Oh, I think she is, sir. She always says to take a leaf out of your book. Now you've taught me to read the Bible properly, she's happy.'

As they spoke, the Major was standing with his back to the door so that he did not see his daughter enter the parlour. Although her dark hair was hidden under a lace-fringed mobcap, Tom thought Megan had never looked lovelier. She glanced over her father's shoulder at him and put a finger to her lips so that he would not betray her presence.

Major Meredith continued, 'You seem to understand what I've tried to do for you, lad, and it's a great happiness to me...'

'And it would be a great happiness to me, father, if you would buy me a flute,' Megan interrupted.

'What? Bring an end to my quiet life!' her father laughed. 'Last week it was a harp. What will it be next, my wild child?'

'But the Reverend Thomas has promised to teach me how to play so that I can accompany the hymns in church, father,' Megan protested.

The Major was taken aback by this reply. He thought for a moment and said, 'In that case, my dear, I'll give careful consideration to the idea. What do you think, Tom?'

The servant felt Megan's cornflower-blue eyes upon him. He played anxiously with his flaxen hair but could not control the heat which flushed his face. 'You've taught me that the more skills we've got, the better, sir. When work's finished for the day, it would be pleasant to sit and listen to a melody or two on the flute.'

Megan gazed at Tom with admiration shining in her eyes. Her father roared, 'A good answer! It seems we'll all be dancing to a flute's beat before long.'

The unexpected echo of hooves and then a horse whinnying brought an end to their conversation. Major Meredith peered outside into the afternoon gloom and his face tightened with anxiety. 'It's a trooper from our local defence force, the Fishguard

Fencibles. He's making such haste that I fear trouble is afoot.'

The private – who wore a striped red jacket, a slouch hat bearing the motto *Ich Dien* and white breeches – entered and barked, 'Sir... The Governor of Fishguard Fort has sent me to warn you that French warships have moored off Carreg Wastad... Enemy troops appear ready to disembark... You're advised to effect an immediate escape inland or to the south.

'We've less than one hundred men and the French are only a short march from here... You and your family must hurry, sir!'

Without further ado, the sweating soldier saluted and swept from their presence to raise the alarm elsewhere.

'Abandon Pentower? Never!' the Major thundered. 'In the old tower, with my sporting guns and pistols beside me, the French will find they've bitten off more than they can chew. They won't take my home without a fight!'

'No, father!' Megan cried. 'We must do as the trooper said. Your life is more precious to me than all the farms in Wales!'

'I shall be safe here, my dear. Dai Williams and Huw, the blacksmith, will stay with me, I'm sure. They love this place almost as much as I do. But everyone else must leave at once.

'Tom, you will take Megan across country to Fishguard. You know the route well enough to find your way, even in the dark. Go home first, and then take your mother to the Fort. The Governor, Gwynne

Vaughan, is a brave man and will see that you come to no harm. Colonel Knox will probably establish his command post there so it's much the safest place for you all. Hurry! The French will be here soon.'

'I won't leave you, father!' Megan declared. 'I may only be seventeen, but I'm enough of a Welsh woman to deal with those Frenchies!'

Tom's eyes glittered proudly as she spoke.

Major Meredith frowned. 'You're young and the world is still yours to play with, my dear. I won't risk your future.' He turned and stared at his servant, 'If I'm any judge of character, this young man would give his life for you.'

'That I would, sir.'

The Master of Pentower patted the youth on the back and said, 'Don't forget your promise, lad. But remember that all the courage and daring in the world are useless without intelligence and endurance. Take no risks with my darling daughter. A dead hero is no use to me.'

With that, he gave Megan a last tender kiss and he shook Tom's hand vigorously. 'You've a dark, stony path ahead of you. Be off now, my pretty pair. And may God save you!'

EIGHT

FLIGHT

The winter wind began to bite. Shuttered and barred, Pentower disappeared into the darkness. When a cloud crossed the moon, Megan grabbed Tom's arm and did not let it go.

'If we take the coast road,' he suggested, 'we should be able to see where the French ships are moored and if their troops are ashore yet. I'm sure Colonel Knox will be grateful for any intelligence we can gather on our way.'

'But, if the French have landed, they will surely take that very path,' Megan argued. 'Father said we should cut across the fields.'

'We can't think only of our safety at such a time, Miss Megan. Your father has stayed to defend Pentower when he could have fled for his life. Don't be afraid! I promise we'll do nothing rash. The cloak of night will hide us. And even the Frenchies wouldn't harm an unarmed lady. Come, let's go.'

Hand in hand, Tom and Megan stumbled into the night. Vague, disturbing scuffles caused them to stop and listen several times. When an owl hooted, their hearts jumped in their chests. Though his feet felt cold and damp, Tom began to sweat under his greatcoat.

No sooner had they staggered onto the rutted, earth track, than they saw indistinct figures in the distance.

'Down!' Tom whispered urgently. They slithered into a dank ditch, with foul water at the bottom. Hardly daring to breathe, the youngsters waited.

On the cheerless wind, Welsh voices drifted towards them. When they realised that this was a group of local people fleeing for their lives, they clambered out of hiding and confronted them.

'Where are you going?' Tom demanded.

'Out of our way!' a bald-headed man shouted at them. '*Mae'r Frenchies yn dod*! They'll be here at any time. Get yourself 'ome, and tell your Da to bury his valuables and 'ead inland. That's what we're all doing.'

'My Da was drowned in a storm at sea years ago,' Tom replied coolly. 'And we're heading for Fishguard where my Mam lives.'

A woman, who had a child tucked into her shawl and a bulging sack over her shoulder, cried, 'No, *bach*, you mustn't do that! The Frenchies are in Fishguard! It will be burnt to the ground by morning!'

'Colonel Knox and his Fencibles will protect us,' Megan insisted.

'Don't place too much faith in Knox and 'is band of drunken louts,' the man advised. 'The officers like parading in their fancy uniforms for the benefit of young ladies like you but, when they faces being maimed or killed, they're as like to turn and run as stand and fight. The infantry are armed with scythes and broomsticks! What chance 'ave they got against experienced French troops? Be sensible! Throw in your lot with us.'

The youngsters stared into each other's eyes, but Megan remained defiant. 'No, we'll do as my father instructed.'

Tom smiled and nodded in agreement. 'Thank you for the offer, but we must be on our way.'

The man shook his pate. 'You must both be *twp!*' With that, he bustled off as fast as his spindly legs would carry him.

A French longboat scraped onto sand and James Bowen leapt ashore followed by Lieutenant St Leger and twenty-five grenadiers. They scrambled up the steep cliffs. In their heavy, woollen uniforms and crossbelts, they were gasping for breath by the time they reached the top.

'Trehowel farm is only a mile or so from here,' Bowen panted. 'Mortimer's face will be a picture when he sees me again.'

Gobbets of sweat stood out on his forehead in spite of the chilly breeze, and a violent gleam appeared in his eyes. 'For years, I served that man. In all weathers, I slaved for him. But he never gave me a chance to better myself. He was the biggest humbug who ever walked God's earth. When I arrive in such company, he won't be looking down his long nose at me!'

'Well, now's yer chance, Bowen,' said the Irishman. 'In France, the aristocrats have been hunted out of the land or had their heads chopped off. It's time to do likewise here. We shall take the land from the owning classes and give it to the peasants. There'll be no more touching yer forelock to the Squire. The world is about to be turned upside down.'

Soon, Bowen thought, he would be seated beside the fire in his former master's place. He turned up his collar and grinned.

Tom and Megan struggled to keep pace with the tattered clouds but, as they neared Carreg Wastad Point, the wind abated and the sky cleared. They could see four monstrous French warships moored off the headland. In the melancholy moonlight, even the murderous cannon, poking out of their black ports, were clearly visible.

'There's a longboat full of soldiers being rowed ashore right now,' Tom gasped. 'Can you see them?'

'Oh, yes! The moon's so bright and the sea so calm that God must be asleep,' Megan replied. 'When the Frenchies tried to invade Ireland, such storms and winds arose that it was impossible for them to land and do any mischief.'

'That's only because they don't have a decent seaman amongst them!' Tom declared. 'Well, it seems *we* shall have to protect ourselves.'

Megan stared at the silhouetted ships and realised that the future was very bleak. She muttered, 'I can't bear to think of those filthy barbarians strutting through our streets, sleeping in our beds and violating our people.'

She tugged her cloak tighter and continued, 'Come, Tom, we've seen enough. The enemy is already landing its troops and weapons. While the Frenchies are climbing the cliffs, they can't defend themselves. We must get to Fishguard and urge Colonel Knox to attack at once.'

No sooner had she uttered these words than Megan let go of Tom's hand and moaned in dismay. They had been staring out to sea so intently that they had not noticed obscure shapes looming out of the darkness. French soldiers, scowling and growling in a fearsome fashion, surrounded them. Tom felt a hand grab his shoulder. When he turned and looked into James Bowen's eyes, he shuddered and shrank back.

'I know this little rat,' Bowen sneered. 'He's of no account, but the girl is Megan Meredith, daughter of the Master of Pentower.' He gave her a mocking bow and continued, 'Still giving yourself airs, eh? I was never good enough for the likes of you, was I?

'Your father would never do anything to harm a hair on your head. You'll make a pretty bargaining counter, *annwyl*!'

NINE

PANIC AT PICTON CASTLE

A grey-haired man, leaning heavily on a silver-handled stick, limped along the shadowy corridors of Picton Castle. Behind his lined forehead, a drum seemed to be beating a tattoo.

'Damn this headache!' he cursed. 'And damn all French republicans!'

When Lord Milford first heard news of the invasion, his knees had almost buckled. As Lord Lieutenant, he was responsible for the defence of the county but, in truth, he had little idea of what to do beyond raise the alarm. He was in his fifties, too old and infirm to command an army in the field.

His natural instinct had been to summon assistance. Hours ago, he had sent an urgent note to Lord Cawdor at his home in Stackpole Court.

'John Campbell is the man for a crisis,' he had told his wife. 'He may be a farmer at heart, but he's the shrewdest man in Pembrokeshire. And I doubt there's a braver one. I think, my dear, I should place him in charge of the military.'

Long past midnight, the first Baron Cawdor's dramatic ride through the wintry countryside ended and his horse's hooves clattered onto the courtyard cobbles. Though his thighs were chafed after hours in the saddle, he hurried into the castle's warmth to discuss no less an issue than the defence of the realm. But he was dismayed to find Lord Milford in a state of indecision which bordered upon panic.

Cawdor strode towards the fireplace and began to thaw his frozen fingers. He realised that it was his duty to restore some order and calm so, in a deep and reassuring voice, he said, 'My lord, we know Colonel Knox is already at Fishguard with his Fencibles, and Lieutenant Cole has mustered the Cardigan Militia which, as luck would have it, are serving in the county. They are marching as we speak. And though they're only tradesmen and tenant-farmers, the Pembroke Volunteers, under Captain Ackland's command, are keen to give the French a bloody nose.

'In addition to the infantry, we have two of the finest troops of cavalry at our disposal – your own Dungleddy Gentlemen and my Castlemartin Yeomanry.

'Furthermore, my lord,' he continued, 'there are several merchant ships and two revenue-cutters at anchor in Milford Haven. They should provide us with at least a hundred able-bodied seamen. Soon we'll have five hundred or more under arms. It will be enough.'

In his brushed uniform, with its gleaming buttons and gold epaulettes, Cawdor made a powerful impression upon Lord Milford, who breathed a heavy sigh of relief. He dabbed a silk handkerchief at his damp brow and said, 'My dear fellow, you've put new heart into me! You're a credit to your distinguished kith and kin. If you would accept overall command of our forces, I should be eternally grateful.'

Milford tapped his leg and added, 'As you can see, I'm not the man I was. This wretched gout renders me of little more use than a cripple so I won't be able to take a part in any action.

'Various messages have arrived confirming that the French fleet has moored off Carreg Wastad Point. Their troops have disembarked and occupied much of the Pencaer peninsula. At all costs, they must not be allowed to take Fishguard. You'll be outnumbered, but regular troops will arrive shortly. Contain the French for a couple of days and victory will be ours!'

Milford's strategy was a simple one which suited Cawdor very well. He ran his fingers through his sandy-coloured hair and said, 'I should be honoured to accept such a commission, my lord. If you would be good enough to confirm my appointment in writing, I shall make Colonel Colby of the Pembrokeshire Militia, my second-in-command. His experience and energy will be invaluable.

'I think the French have underestimated the resentment and hostility of the local people to this incursion. They are rallying to our cause with great enthusiasm. And you may rest assured that I'll do everything in my power to ensure the enemy does not head inland.'

'Oh, I'm sure you will, my dear fellow! My thanks, my sincerest thanks.'

Lord Milford pulled himself to his feet and winced as he put his full weight on his right knee, but a grin flickered on his lips as he hobbled across to a bronze inkstand which sat on an ornate table in the middle of the portrait-lined room.

'Whilst I busy myself with pen and ink, help yourself to the brandy. The decanter and glasses are on the tallboy. I think I shall write a note to the Lord Lieutenant of Carmarthen first, asking him to send as many men as he can. By noon, there should be a veritable army of volunteers for you to command. And we shall both have done our duty by King George.'

'Aye, my lord,' Cawdor agreed, through a wry smile, 'and let us hope that this raid is not the first of many.' Nevertheless, he added a lusty, 'God save the King!'

TEN

ATTACK ON PENTOWER

Trehowel was locked and deserted. John Mortimer had ordered his servants to get away as best they could, whilst he saddled a horse and rode to a neighbouring farm at Llanwnwr. Behind him, he left a kitchen groaning with food and drink in readiness for his forthcoming wedding.

French soldiers approached the dark farmhouse warily but, when their knocks went unanswered, they battered the door open with musket butts and boots.

'Stand aside!' St Leger shouted to his men. Well aware that they were at liberty for the first time in weeks and sensed the chance for plunder, he was not sure that they would obey him. 'If anyone enters that building without my permission, I'll shoot him!' he yelled.

But the grenadiers laughed in the commanding officer's boyish face, raised their muskets and pointed them straight at him. '*Au contraire,*' one rejoined, 'we shall shoot you, if you stand in our way!'

Tom and Megan watched in horror as St Leger was

forced to beg, 'For pity's sake, don't shoot! Remember that there's a young lady present!'

The youngsters sighed with relief when the invaders turned around and stormed into the house and began helping themselves to all the bread, meat, cheese and wine which they could find. Lieutenant St Leger, distraught at their mutinous disloyalty, headed into the safety of the darkness and left his men to get drunk.

But James Bowen remained sober. As he crammed chunks of bread and cheese into his mouth, he watched the two hand-bound captives like a lynx.

Within a couple of hours, the kitchen was littered with snoring soldiers. Only a few of the grenadiers remained in possession of their senses. One of these, a former schoolmaster named Gaspard, spoke fairly fluent English.

Bowen sidled up to him and confided, 'This place is nothing compared to Pentower. Its Master hoards a stash of gold guineas in a stone tower there. His daughter swears that he's fled already, but I know she's lying.

'Meredith isn't like Mortimer; he won't run from anyone or anything. If I'm any judge of character, he'll protect his property – whatever the cost. But, with a few musket-balls, we'll despatch him into the hereafter. And then, you and I will be rich!'

'*Bien, mon ami! Bien,*' Gaspard muttered. He belched, then a slurred smile crossed his lips. 'And maybe we can teach *la mademoiselle galloise* to like you!'

'First we'll celebrate with a meal of prime Welsh

beef,' Bowen said. He cracked his knuckles and grinned at Megan. 'I've not had a decent meal in months.'

'Open up, Meredith! Open this blasted door!' Bowen yelled. His face was thunderous and his fists were clenched. A shiver ran through Tom and Megan as they saw his vengeful features. He looked barely human.

Pentower's only answer was silence.

'When I give the signal,' Bowen ordered, 'break down that door. Don't touch Meredith. He's mine. Nobody must kill him but me!'

Suddenly, the bolts caved in and the door crashed open. Bowen and his French ally rushed into the lifeless house. Shuttered from the moonlight, darkness brought them to a halt. Only a sullen glow came from a fire which was dying in the hearth.

'Stay here and I'll fetch some candles,' Bowen said.

Eerie shadows stalked across the panelled parlour marking his return.

'Meredith will be holed up in the tower with his gold like the miser he is,' he sneered, 'but we'll check upstairs, just to be sure.'

The attackers' boots clattered up the wooden staircase. At the top, Bowen stopped and stared straight into his Master's eyes! Instinctively, he drew back, but only for a moment. The Major's disparaging look came from a harmless concoction of oils and canvas.

Swiftly regaining his composure, Bowen

unsheathed a knife from his waistband and slashed the painted face. The Major's blue eyes were sliced apart, his creamy-pink throat was torn open and a final stab punctured his heart. All this, Bowen thought, was just a foretaste of what was to come in the flesh!

'It's deserted, *mon ami!*' Gaspard called.

'I thought he'd be hiding in the tower,' Bowen replied. 'Let's go. The wooden floors should burn well enough. Gold coins will survive a fire but Meredith won't. When we're done, either we'll find his charred corpse or we'll drill him with musket-fire as he tries to escape the flames.'

Not for the first time, Bowen leered lecherously at Megan. 'Don't worry, *annwyl*, I'll take good care of you when your father's dead.'

'No!' Megan shrieked. 'You can't set fire to the tower! I'll do anything you want... anything. But you must promise to let my father live!'

'Oh, you'll do anything I say, whatever happens to your father. You seem to forget that I give the orders now,' Bowen sneered.

A small pile of gunpowder exploded in a yellow flash. Then the doorway to the tower blossomed with reddish smoke and there was a roar as the fire took hold. Megan screamed and a torrent of tears flowed down her face.

Bowen, the flames reflecting in his excited eyes, grinned horribly. But, when he looked at Megan and saw her head leaning against Tom's shoulder for comfort, he leapt at the youth and punched him in the stomach. Winded and breathless, Tom doubled up in agony and fell to his knees. He clutched at his belly as if trying to squeeze out the pain.

'Keep your bloody hands off my woman, boyo!' Bowen snarled. 'As soon as I've done with Meredith, it'll be your turn!'

Then he threw a second punch, but Tom swayed back so that the clenched fist hissed past him. Enraged by this miss, Bowen lowered his skull and butted Tom's head with such force that he was knocked senseless. They left his body stretched out on the cold, damp grass.

Major Meredith's face was grave as he watched smoke drift up the spiral staircase. He stood shoulder-to-shoulder with Dai, the coachman, and Huw, the blacksmith, on the first floor of the ancient tower.

Centuries ago, the coiled stone steps had been built to make an all-out assault impossible. Now, in 1797, their clever design still ensured that the unfortunate soldier who led any French charge would have his head blown apart as soon as it appeared in the sights of the Major's primed pistols. The second and third soldiers would meet a similar fate, but then there would be no time to reload, so the fourth and fifth would only encounter swords and scythes. Major Meredith and his loyal servants awaited death bravely.

Gaspard hoped the explosion, fire and smoke would cause panic in Pentower's defenders. He clumped up the narrow steps and, momentarily, glimpsed three figures towering above him. Several shots rang out and he felt a fierce, hot pain in his chest. Blood began to froth in his mouth. He fell backwards and looked to Bowen for help, but his Welsh ally was nowhere to be seen.

The once-popular teacher staggered into the welcome arms of the cold night air as a dreadful clamminess engulfed his body. He rolled and lurched like a drunken man for a few more steps. Then he tottered forward, gave a last grunt, and plunged to the earth in an eternal sleep.

'Go up to the battlements and try to see what's happening, Huw,' the Major ordered. 'Surely there must be more French troops out there... unless that was a lone deserter who mistook the tower for a safe refuge.'

The stocky blacksmith was soon peering into the inky darkness but he could neither see nor hear anything untoward. He descended the steep steps warily and reported his blank findings.

'It's no use!' the Major snapped in exasperation. 'I can't bear this inaction any longer. My place is alongside Colonel Knox. He's raw and might benefit from my military experience. If the French burn Pentower to the ground, so be it.

'By now, volunteers from all over Pembrokeshire should be on their way to Fishguard. Tom and Megan will be there already. It's time to join them. Are you with me, lads?'

Both of his relieved servants nodded in enthusiastic agreement.

ELEVEN

JEMIMA

Tom could see a wedge of the moon and stars shining above him. For a few frightening moments, he had no idea where he was. He only knew there was an insistent buzzing noise in his ears and a dreadful pain scything through his head and that he had never felt so wretched before.

The freezing night air swiftly brought him back to his senses and he recalled where he was and why. He began to shiver. The French had stolen his greatcoat earlier and, as his hands were still tied, he could not hug himself for comfort and warmth. He was chilled to the bone.

'Help me... Help me...' he moaned.

But no aid came. He was alone. Spurred on by this appalling realisation, Tom forced his body into a sitting position by wriggling like a woodlouse. He dug his heels into the earth and pushed himself along on his bottom until his back leaned against the nearest tree. Using this as a support, the youth levered himself upright. He tried stamping his feet to get the blood moving again but this caused the ache in his skull to worsen and his stomach to churn so that he vomited. The sordid mess gave him some temporary relief.

Then he peered around. Smoke rising from the ancient tower made him shudder. Where was Megan?

Dazed and bleary-eyed, Tom staggered forward. As he approached the tower, he stumbled and pitched forward onto his face. He had not fallen over a log, as he had at first supposed, but the lifeless body of a man!

The corpse lay face-down on the earth. Tom had to push unceremoniously with both feet to twist and turn the body. With an undignified flop, its pale features were revealed. A deathly chill ran through his bones as he recognised the ugly grimace caked in dried blood.

'Gaspard!' he grunted. 'Thank God.'

Then Tom noticed the dead man's flintlock musket, its bayonet still fixed, was lying a few yards away. For the first time that night, he gave a grim smile of satisfaction. Though scratched and torn by rubbing the tightly bound ropes against the sharpened metal, his wrists were soon free. He celebrated by tearing a leather pouch, full of powder and shot, from the dead man's belt and snatching the musket. Thus armed, Tom set off.

'If Gaspard's dead,' he muttered to himself, 'perhaps the Major and Megan are safe and sound in Pentower.'

But, when he scoured the house, it was as empty as a skeleton's skull. His disappointment was almost tangible. Though he felt isolated and afraid, he lit a lantern and headed into the dark.

As he neared the tower, the air became heavy with the acrid smell of smoke and gunpowder. But it soon became clear that the fire had done little damage beyond destroying the doorway. When Tom entered the circular room which constituted the ground floor, it was also deserted.

Coughing like an old hag, he stepped onto the spiral staircase which led to the second storey. Holding the lantern aloft, Tom looked around. There was no evidence of any commotion having happened here. A bare wooden table and two dusty chairs stood mutely in the middle of the room as they had always done.

'Where is everyone?' Tom asked himself, but he got no answer.

He scrambled downstairs and began running towards Trehowel. Thoughts of his mother, lonely and frightened in Fishguard, flitted through his mind. Should he return home? But when he compared his mother's situation with Megan's, his duty was obvious.

He stumbled through the dark undergrowth, grasping the musket tightly. A dreadful desperation drove him onwards. The moon gave just enough light to see the silhouettes of trees and shrubs as he swept past. Only when loud singing and coarse laughter reached his ears, did he pause for a deep breath.

Tom inched his way forward in the shadows, fearing what he would find. He froze and swallowed hard when Trehowel's front door opened and a grenadier stepped out. But the soldier swayed drunkenly towards the chicken-coop and fired his musket into the squawking fowls. Shouting and cheering greeted him as he returned with an unfortunate hen draped over his arm.

Like a thief in the night, Tom edged his way around the farmhouse until he reached the kitchen window. Beads of cold sweat crept down his neck and onto his back. He steadied his breathing and then, very cautiously, peered into the room which was lit by a copper oil-lamp. Several soldiers slouched and sprawled across the table, but there was no sign of Megan. Tom clenched his fists in frustration and cursed.

Suddenly, a Frenchman raised his head, thumped his fist on the table and growled at the boyish face framed by the window. Tom had lingered too long! He turned and raced across the farmyard. Some muskets crackled and balls of lead hissed and hummed past his ears.

'Sweet Jesus, save me!' he cried out.

Blindly, he crashed his way through gorse and bracken, ignoring the painful scratches of thorns and brambles. When his lungs felt about to burst, he stopped running. He examined his unscathed body and could scarcely believe his good fortune. As he sucked down ragged gasps of air, he gave a silent prayer of thanks.

But his contentment was short-lived. Through the frosty air came the sound of whispering. An involuntary shiver ran down his spine, then his body went rigid and the hairs on his neck tingled. How had drunken Frenchies tracked him? In a desperate effort to control his misty panting, he clenched his teeth so hard that his jaw ached.

Then a deep voice demanded, '*Pwy sy 'na?*'

Though he did not speak much Welsh, Tom recognised the ancient language and its speaker's gruff tone. His shoulders sagged with relief and he called out, 'Jemima! Jemima Nicholas! It's Tom – Tom Phillips from Fishguard!'

A strapping woman, carrying a pitchfork, emerged from the darkness. Jemima was the local cobbler and a well-known figure in the area. She had a reputation for being stronger and more short-tempered than most men but Tom had always found her warm and friendly. Behind her stood a few followers also armed with pitchforks, billhooks or newly-sharpened scythes.

'What are you doing out here? There are Frenchies everywhere!' Tom exclaimed.

'Oh, I know that, *bach*! But the Frogs are a bunch of fops and dancers, and I mean to bang a few of their heads together before the sun rises! Why aren't you at home with your Mam? I saw her not two hours ago.'

'So she's safe then?'

'Yes, she's fine where she is. Volunteers from all over the county are heading for the Fort as we speak. The Frenchies may outnumber us, but they'll only take Fishguard over our dead bodies!'

Tom grimaced and said, 'Let's hope it won't come to that... Have you seen James Bowen, Jemima?'

'Jim Bowen? Wasn't he transported to Australia for horse- rustling?'

'Well, that's what I thought. But it turns out he's

a French spy! And, even worse, he's kidnapped Megan Meredith! I dread to think what he means to do with her. I've been to Pentower and the French headquarters at Trehowel and seen neither hide nor hair of them.'

A look of horror crossed Jemima's face as she swore loudly in Welsh. 'Well, we're not going to let a traitor harm pretty Miss Megan, are we? Unless Bowen wants to be shot as a deserter, he'll have to return to Trehowel soon, so they can't be far away. Come with us, *bach*. We'll find them for you. And, when we do,' Jemima paused to spit on the ground, 'Jim Bowen'll wish he'd never been born!

'The only shelter between Pentower and Trehowel is the forge,' she continued. 'If he wants his wicked way with Miss Megan, that's the place he'll likely choose.'

'Hurry, Jemima!' Tom urged. 'She's not safe in that beast's hands!'

TWELVE

A SHOT
IN THE DARK

The ghostly moon shone from a cloudless sky and the night grew colder. The grass began to crunch under Tom's feet but he was in such haste that he barely noticed.

The small band of rescuers slithered down the slippery path which led to the forge and, sure enough, a sliver of light glowed between the ill-fitting shutters.

'Steady, *bach*,' Jemima whispered, as she grabbed Tom's shoulder.

'Jim Bowen may be a traitor but he's not deaf! We must take him by surprise. Stay here. Leave this to us.'

'Kiss me, damn you!' Bowen demanded. 'I've been waiting for those cherry lips long enough.'

Megan began to slink backwards, praying that her captor was no more than a phantom in the vilest nightmare. But she did not awaken. Instead, she found her back pressed against the forge's anvil with the villain's rancid breath filling her nostrils.

'God help me… God help me…' she beseeched, but Bowen's cruel mouth ended her prayers. He forced his rough tongue against hers so hard that she had to gasp for air. She could feel his hands crawling over her body and tearing at her dress. The forge began to spin and swirl. She felt faint. Instinctively, Megan fought the blackness but, as consciousness prepared for flight, she heard a crash and the door was flung open.

'Enough of that, Jim Bowen!' Jemima yelled. 'Keep your filthy hands to yourself!'

Tom peered through a gap in the rotten shutters and watched, in horror, as Bowen pulled out a knife and held it to Megan's throat. To remain outside doing nothing was the hardest thing Tom had ever done. He wanted to rush inside, snatch his mistress into his arms and leap to safety together.

'One step closer, Jemima Nicholas, and I'll slit her from ear to ear. Get back! You know I've nothing to lose…'

While Bowen made his evil threats, Tom rammed some black powder and a lead ball down the stolen musket's barrel. Then he opened the flashpan and filled it with a little more powder from the leather pouch just as he had seen Major Meredith do when out shooting pheasants.

For a moment or two there was silence. Then Jemima shouted, 'Wait! Wait! Hurt Miss Megan and you're a dead man!'

'Don't you dare threaten me!' Bowen yelled. 'Put your arms down. Now!'

As Jemima signalled to her followers to drop their makeshift weapons, Tom could hear his heart thumping. In desperation, he raised and cocked the musket, and took aim at the traitor's temple. Then he pulled the trigger and felt the brass butt kick into his shoulder.

An explosion shattered the night air. The shot whistled past Bowen's ear causing him to recoil and let the knife slip from his grasp. But he regathered his senses quickly and clambered through the window at the back of the forge before a shocked Jemima could pick up her pitchfork and charge at him.

Megan slumped across the anvil and began to weep uncontrollably. She was dishevelled, her dress was torn and her face was scratched. Jemima took the sobbing girl in her powerful arms for comfort.

'There, there, *annwyl*, you're safe now. We won't let that fiend near you ever again. That's right, have a good cry. You'll feel the better for it. Has he harmed you in any way?'

Megan shook her head. 'No, you were in time,' she whispered.

But when Tom shuffled into the forge, Jemima's voice took on a less sympathetic tone.

'What a dangerous trick to play, *bach*! You could've blown Miss Megan's brains out! Or that blackguard's knife could have jerked up into her throat as easily as it fell to the floor. You're a lucky lad, Tom Phillips.'

'What else could I do?' he protested. 'Bowen was about to kill her!'

'Well, that's true,' Jemima agreed. Then a smile played around the corners of her mouth. 'And your shot in the dark turned out well in the end, I suppose. Now I must get after that fleet-footed devil and make sure he doesn't escape.

'When Miss Megan feels steady enough to walk, take her home to your Mam's. She'll care for you both. Steer clear of roads and paths. Go across country and, this time, do as you're told!'

One by one, Jemima's companions followed her into the darkness until Tom and Megan were alone. The boy's eyes had become accustomed to the miserly lantern-light and he noticed a little colour returning to his mistress's pale face. He stared adoringly at her, but she just looked to the floor.

He was not sure what to do next. She only had to raise a finger and he would go through hell and high water for her. Above all things, he wanted to clasp her close and console her with a kiss. But Miss Megan was a lady, and he was a servant – not a knight from Camelot. It was madness and dishonourable even to think of such a thing. And Tom knew his place.

Eventually, he held out his hand and was gratified to feel her soft, slender fingers entwine with his. A hot flush crossed his face when she looked up at him. Those sapphire eyes were hypnotic.

They set off for Fishguard once again, praying that they would not encounter any more French troops but, as they neared the towering crags of Carn Wnda, hawk-eyed Tom spotted small groups of enemy soldiers sitting around gorse fires or wandering about aimlessly. Several heart-stopping times, the pair were forced to drop to their knees in the bracken and listen until the sounds of movement passed.

Then they scrambled down the steep hill and headed through the small village of Goodwick which was ghostly quiet. The streets and houses and gardens were deserted. Everyone had fled. But they saw no more French troops, so they crossed the bridge and wearily tramped up the winding road into Fishguard.

The town square was a mass of flaring torches held aloft by local folk, many of whom carried long poles topped with scythes in their other hands. A small force of about seventy Fencibles, mostly armed with muskets, stood to attention in front of The Royal Oak inn. Before them stood Lieutenant Colonel Thomas Knox, young and splendid-looking in his scarlet uniform.

But grave mutterings about the inexperienced commander soon reached their ears. Earlier, Colonel Knox had ordered Ensign Bowen and his volunteers back from Goodwick Sands to the Fort. The local Fencibles had been eager to drive the enemy into the sea, but Knox had feared their lack of numbers and the advent of darkness would have resulted in a disaster. Though scouts had been sent out and sentries posted, there would be no attack until reinforcements and daylight arrived. Orders were shouted and the soldiers about-turned and began to march off for a few hours' rest.

Tom also made to move when, without warning, Gaspard's musket was ripped from his grasp. A burly sergeant growled, 'I don't know how you laid hands on this, lad, but our need of it is greater than yours. When we've done with the Frogs, we'll return it to you – if you're lucky!'

Before the youth could make any protest, he recognised his mother's voice calling his name.

'Mam, oh Mam, it's so good to see you again! Yes, we're both unharmed but we've such a tale to tell...'

'You should be very proud of your son, Mistress Phillips,' Megan interrupted. 'He's a hero! Only an hour or so ago, he saved my life. All of Fishguard will be talking about him tomorrow, and I'm sure my father will reward his bravery well.'

Tom glowed with pride as he listened to Megan's tribute but, when she stood on tiptoe to kiss his bloodied cheek, his heart felt as if it would burst with joy.

'Upon my soul!' Mistress Phillips gasped, as she gave her much-loved son a hug which took his breath away. She was grateful that her only child was maturing into such a fine young man under Major Meredith's guidance.

'Well, thank the Lord you're both safe. But where is your father, my dear?'

Miss Megan suddenly looked distraught. 'I don't know! He said he'd go to the old tower with Huw and Dai. But James Bowen and a French devil tried to set fire to the place. The flames didn't take a hold, and when Tom searched inside there was no sign of them. So it seems they escaped. I prayed they'd be here already. Haven't you seen them?'

'No, the arrival of a military man such as your

father would have been greeted with loud cheers. Of that, I'm certain.' She paused and then continued, 'Did my ears deceive me or did you say that James Bowen is with the French?'

It was Tom's turn to interrupt. 'Yes, Mam, it's as if he's come back from the dead to haunt us. He's a traitor! And he wants to butcher us all!'

'Calm yourself, dear. Inflaming people's fears is not what we need right now,' Mistress Phillips insisted.

Tom did as he was bidden, but he thought his mother would be a lot less tranquil and sanguine when he told her the full story of his adventures.

'We can leave the likes of Jim Bowen to Colonel Knox. Let's go home and warm ourselves before the fire. You both look done in.'

The snug kitchen had a womb-like effect upon the youngsters. Suddenly, they felt secure and comfortable. Before Mistress Phillips could bid them a 'Good night', they were asleep.

THIRTEEN

TATE AT TREHOWEL

'On your feet,' James Bowen whispered into Barry St Leger's ear. 'It's time to show those lousy villains who's in charge here.'

The young man from Limerick was slouched, head in hands, a short distance from Trehowel farmhouse.

'Dear God, yez nearly frightened the life out of me! Where have yer been for the past couple of hours? I could've done with yer help. And where's the pretty Welsh lass?'

Bowen tapped his nose with a finger and answered, 'That's my business, boyo. But nothing will get done by sitting here and sighing. Your men are too drunk to defy you any longer. Just tell them that Tate will be along at any minute and they'll fall into line.'

St Leger recovered himself and forced a grin. 'Are they all drunk?'

'Probably. Let's go and see. Keep your voice and hands steady and you'll soon have their knees trembling.'

The mutiny was, indeed, at an end. For a moment or two, the dazed grenadiers were dismayed to see their officer and his Welsh henchman return, but a strange relief gripped them when it became evident that it suited everyone to act as if nothing untoward had happened. By the time General Tate and his senior officers arrived, some order and tidiness had been restored, though a pungent whiff of brandy hung in the air.

The white-haired commander had snatched some sleep on the cliff-top at Carreg Wastad, but his shoulders were round with fatigue and disappointment. Though the work parties had landed barrels of gunpowder, boxes of handgrenades and a sheet of ball cartridges, he had watched helplessly as an overladen boat had capsized and sent all his four-pounder cannon and eight men into the dark depths of Cardigan Bay. Their desperate, futile screams were still ringing in his ears.

And his conviction that the local peasantry would flock to the French side had already been undermined by reports that they were resisting or running away.

'Have any Welshmen rallied to our cause?' he asked.

His officers shook their heads. 'Either they flee, or they fight us, sir,' said one. 'They don't seem to want a revolution, after all.'

Tate sighed and stared at James Bowen. 'Where's the highest spot near here?'

The turncoat pointed to a place on the map which was spread across the kitchen table. 'Carn Wnda. You'll have a good view of the whole area from up there. It can only be climbed from one side, so it's like a fortress.'

'In that case, Lieutenant, take your men to the summit and raise the tricolour,' Tate ordered St Leger. 'By noon, we shall have our troops stretched from Carn Wnda in the north to Carn Gelli in the south. An attack upon such a strong position would be madness.'

The dying squeals of a stuck pig and loud laughter interrupted Tate's commands. 'And get those men under control before you leave!' he snorted.

A look of apprehension crossed St Leger's winsome face as he hurried from the room.

Another Irishman, Captain Robert Morrison, who acted as the general's interpreter, waited for the door to close and said, 'Sir, the men are half-starved. Will you allow the dispatch of foraging parties to search for food? They should find plenty to eat in the farms round about.'

'Yes, yes, see to it,' Tate muttered tetchily. 'But, for God's sake, try to keep those rogues and ruffians sober! And take any horses and carts to carry our supplies and ammunition. General Hoche's orders were to march for Liverpool without delay. We can't afford to get bogged down here.'

What General Tate did not know was that, a few weeks earlier, a Portuguese coaster carrying a cargo of wine had been wrecked off the Pembrokeshire coast and most of the local farmhouses were now well-stocked with looted port. Within a few hours, most of the French marauders were rendered senseless by too much alcohol or ill by half-cooked food.

In the course of the night and the following morning, the Pencaer peninsula was stripped of its livestock, some of it eaten raw, so desperate were the men of the Black Legion.

'And what about Commodore Castagnier, sir? He is anxious to weigh anchor and return to France,' asked the ex-aristocrat, Jacques Phillipe Le Brun.

'I am well aware of that, sir,' Tate snapped at his second-in-command. The old republican did not entirely trust the former Baron de Rochemure's loyalty. 'Castagnier will depart when I give him leave to do so and not a second before! Is that understood?'

'*Oui, mon Général,*' replied the Chef de Battalion sheepishly. He was not accustomed to being barked at by his mild-mannered superior.

'What I would give for his forty cannon...' the General added. He slumped into a chair and stared at the fire which, like his lifetime's ambition, was dying in front of him.

FOURTEEN

RETREAT

The frost had thawed and a dreary drizzle greeted the dawn of 23 February, 1797. After a couple of hours' sleep, Major Meredith was standing outside Mistress Phillips' house, anxious to see his beloved daughter but reluctant to disturb her slumbers. The landlord of The Black Bull tavern had reassured him that Megan was safe, all that really mattered.

He rapped his knuckles on the door and Mistress Phillips, dressed in a flannel nightgown, soon appeared.

'Oh, do come out of the cold, Major. Miss Megan is still fast asleep. Sit by the fire and I'll make you some tea.'

Whilst the Major was sipping a fine Indian brew, a tousle-haired figure entered the kitchen. Tom's face lit up when he saw his Master.

'Thank the Lord you're alive, sir!' he gasped. 'When I realised that Jim Bowen had set fire to the old tower, I expected to find your corpse inside! It was such a relief that only Gaspard was dead...'

A frown of confusion crossed the Major's face. 'What on earth do you mean, lad? I thought you and Megan had been safely abed here all night.'

Suddenly, it struck Tom that his Master had no

knowledge of their failure to obey instructions, their capture by the French, nor Megan's horrific ordeal at Bowen's hands. Now that he would have to relate the tale, the Major would be furious with him. At best, he faced dismissal from service at Pentower. At worst, he would be banished from Megan's presence for ever.

The shame-faced youth stared at the stone floor. Dressed only in his nightshirt, he felt very cold. 'No, sir,' he admitted, 'we took the coast road to look for the French fleet and were captured...'

'Dear God, tell me that's a feeble attempt at a jest!' the Major cried out. His face darkened as he demanded, 'I want the truth. No more, nor less.'

Major Meredith drained the teacup to its dregs as he listened, while Tom told his story slowly and thoughtfully, trying not to forget any important details. When he finished, the Master tilted his head forward and fingered his chin. There was an uneasy silence for a time.

Then he said, 'My feelings have never been so confused in all my life. I don't know whether to scold or embrace you!'

The Major's uncertainty gave Tom a spark of optimism and some colour returned to his cheeks.

'I lost my head, sir! I'm ashamed of the way I behaved and apologise for my foolishness.'

'Well, it was wrong of you to ignore my orders,' the Major continued, 'but Megan is asleep on a feather mattress, not cold and lifeless in the forge. For that, I'll always be in your debt, lad.'

The grateful man, dressed in mournful black, crossed

the room and put his hand upon Tom's shoulder. 'At your age, I might have done the same thing. Let's just give thanks that you've both been spared. But none of us is safe yet. The French are still on our doorstep. Shortly, Colonel Knox will be marching the Fencibles into the town square and preparing to attack. The Newport division arrived during the night so he now has 120 men. Lord Cawdor and his Castlemartin Yeomanry should be here by noon. It's high time I joined them.'

'It'll take me but a moment to put on a shirt and breeches, sir,' Tom declared, as a momentary vision of riding into battle together, like some mediaeval knight and squire, flitted through his imagination.

'Oh, no! You've had excitement enough. Stay here and take care of your mother and Megan. My mind won't be easy otherwise.'

Tom knew the Major was tough, but fair. If he made a decision or found fault, there was a good reason for it. So he stood still and bit his lip, in spite of the disappointment which was almost overwhelming him.

Major Meredith could sense his servant's dismay and decided to relent a little. 'On second thoughts, I don't see why you shouldn't all come with me to The Royal Oak. There's to be a Council of War there later which I must attend. Lord Cawdor, one of the most important men in the county, will be present as will Colonel Colby, perhaps the finest soldier I've ever had the privilege of serving.

'But mark my words, lad. You will fire no musket today. If any harm were to come to you now, I dread to think what your mother would do to me!'

Tom and Megan stood with their parents among the crowd lining the road to the town square. Everyone clapped and cheered as the Fishguard Fencibles marched past to the beat of a drum. In their striped, scarlet jackets and slouch hats, they inspired the noisy onlookers with a confidence that was not entirely deserved.

When Colonel Knox saw Meredith, he reined in his horse and leant down to whisper in a confidential fashion. The Major blanched at what was said.

As soon as the young commander rode on, Major Meredith explained, 'Knox says there are probably 1,400 French troops spread across the Pencaer peninsula, and he has less than 200. With such odds, it's too risky to attack. So he's decided to assemble his men outside The Royal Oak and give them some bread, cheese and ale. Then he'll lead them onto the Haverfordwest road to await reinforcements.'

'Retreat? But Colonel Knox has given the order to retreat twice! Only a coward would do such a thing!' Tom sneered.

The Major frowned. 'Knox is a proud man. He wouldn't give such commands lightly. The French outnumber us seven to one. It makes sense to wait for Lord Cawdor. When his cavalry arrive, the balance will begin to tilt in our direction.

'Now, I'll make my way to the inn where I hope to dine before a roaring fire. It seems there will be no action until this afternoon, so I suggest, Mistress Phillips, that you take our children to your home and do likewise.'

Their short walk was interrupted by the sight of boys dancing and jeering and throwing stones at a group of bedraggled Frenchies. Behind them strode a grinning Jemima Nicholas and her companions, their pitchforks aimed menacingly at the captives' backs.

'Jemima!' Tom yelled to make himself heard above the hubbub. 'How did you manage to capture so many?'

'Tipsy Frogs may croak but they don't seem to fight!' she laughed. 'You and Miss Megan would've been more than a match for this feeble crew. They'll all be guests in one of King George's prisons soon enough.

'If you take a stroll up Bigney Hill, you'll be able to see the Frenchies hiding in their burrows like frightened rabbits. You'll get a good view of things from up there.' With that suggestion, Jemima spat some chewed tobacco at her prisoners and moved them on towards the local gaol.

'Oh, please may we go?' Megan pleaded. After her recent ordeal, she had been unusually quiet, but suddenly a familiar gleam shone in her eyes. Tom grinned with pleasure to see that she was a great deal calmer in mind and spirit already. He looked longingly at the young woman beside him as the wintry wind played with her untied hair. The dark angel smiled at him, and he blushed. Though he sensed his heartfelt love was not entirely returned, he was convinced he had begun to earn Megan's devotion.

'Well, the Major wouldn't approve,' Mistress

Phillips replied, 'but I must admit that I'd like to be able to see what's going on. And a lot of women seem to be heading that way. Jemima wouldn't suggest going anywhere dangerous, I'm sure.' She paused to think, then drew her red shawl around her shoulders and tugged her tall, black hat tightly onto her head.

'My curiosity has got the better of my judgement. But I would appreciate it if you did not talk of this diversion with your father, my dear.'

Although the day was dull and dreary, it was not difficult to spy upon the movements of the blue-coated grenadiers on the Pencaer peninsula. Meanwhile, the inexperienced French soldiers peered across the Goodwick Sands at the misty mountain in the distance and saw red-coated figures moving about, and naturally took them to be British soldiers. It was to prove a costly mistake.

The darker uniforms of the Black Legionnaires were more difficult to spot. This was because many of them were, at that very moment, looting and stealing anything they could lay hands upon. Even the church at Llanwnda was raided.

While the invaders stole communion plates the local defenders stripped lead from the roof of St David's Cathedral to fashion musket-balls. The French were in disarray and many of them were openly disobeying orders. Their dreadful behaviour ensured that the Welsh people flocked in droves to support Lord Cawdor, and not General Tate.

FIFTEEN

CASTAGNIER'S FAREWELL

The wind was so slight that the sea looked like a silver salver. On board the *Vengeance*, Commodore Jean Joseph Castagnier was starting to fret. As his cabin rocked gently on the tide, he studied his charts of the Irish Sea. He had completed his part of the invasion and had already stayed longer than he should have done. By now, English frigates would be at sea hunting him. But he needed Tate's permission before he could set sail and he had no idea what fate had befallen the old man.

'To remain here like sitting-ducks is madness,' he said to his senior officers. 'Enseinge Chosel, as commander of our smallest vessel, you will head for Brest to relay the good news that the *Legion Noire* has landed safely. My orders are that the *Vengeance*, *Resistance* and *Constance* are to patrol the Irish coast doing whatever damage we can to merchant shipping. Then we too shall return to France.'

He paused when a young sailor appeared in the doorway and said, 'Sir, the *Chef de Brigade* and the *Chef de Battalion* are approaching in a longboat.'

'Thank God for that,' Castagnier muttered.

The stony look on Tate's face, as he stooped to enter the cabin, told all. His lined features betrayed every one of his seventy years. He was seething with anger and resentment which he could no longer repress.

'General Hoche has given me the devil of an army! Drunkards and scoundrels! What am I to do with such an ill-disciplined rabble? My entire life has been spent dreaming of this moment – leading an army onto British soil. But it has turned into a nightmare in less than a day!'

Though Castagnier sympathised, he had no desire to re-embark a horde of inebriated gaol-birds, probably under British fire. All he desired was to get his ships away safely, and as soon as possible.

'*Mon Général*, I should be obliged if you would sign this deposition confirming that I've carried out my duties in full and have your permission to leave.'

Tate shook his head. 'Before you depart, *mon Commodore*, I'd like to establish a code of signals by which we can communicate should you be required here, in the future.'

Castagnier shrugged his epauletted shoulders. 'But why?' he asked. 'I have no orders to return. You are to march north for Liverpool and I am to set sail for Ireland.'

'Humour me, sir!' Tate snapped. 'There are far more British troops in this area than we ever suspected, and the Welsh peasants refuse to join our revolutionary cause. The truth is that I see little prospect of our breaking out of Pembrokeshire. We may need you to save us from a shameful surrender.'

Castagnier's long eyelashes flickered. He was shocked to hear the word "surrender" already on the General's tongue. He hesitated for a moment, unsure of what to suggest, but he pulled himself together and continued, 'Perhaps Hoche has a follow-up expedition planned. If you'll sign this deposition, sir, I shall gladly set up such a system of signals.'

Tate stared at the cabin floor. Both men knew the Directory in France had lost interest in the *Legion Noire* and that no reinforcements would be sent. There had never been any intention of the French fleet's remaining off Fishguard. After agreeing to an elaborate code of red flags and rockets, Tate and Le Brun reluctantly signed Castagnier's deposition. The Commodore, who had hated every moment of this disastrous expedition, sighed with relief.

Then the disconsolate General was rowed ashore. He clambered onto the rocks at Carreg Wastad and looked out to sea. With due ceremony, he pulled out both his pistols and fired them into the air as a farewell to Castagnier. A salvo of cannon-fire came from the *Vengeance* in an answering salute. Tears dripped down the veteran's face as he watched the French crews raise great shrouds of canvas. The sails caught a breath of breeze and the four ships headed for the horizon.

In all his long life, William Tate had never felt so bereft.

'Oh, dear God! Now what's to become of us?' whispered an appalled Lieutenant St Leger when Captain Morrison informed him of the departure of the fleet. As far as the Irishmen were concerned, they had been left to die.

The news – and with it, panic – spread across the Pencaer peninsula like the Black Death. Even the officers of the *Legion Noire* had not been forewarned of this turn of events.

'Well, I've no wish to dance at the end of an English rope,' said Morrison. 'The General has a soft spot for you, Barry. If you tell him the game's up, I think he might listen. The men think they've been abandoned and are refusing to obey orders already. Soon they'll be completely out of control. It's up to you, my boy. You must persuade Tate to surrender!'

St Leger nodded in agreement. 'Judging by the hundreds of troops and cavalry which I've just watched march down the Haverfordwest road, less than half-a-mile from here, I'd say we've not much time before an attack.'

Morrison interrupted, 'And Captain Tyrrell has reported that there are redcoats stationed on Bigney Hill, so we shall soon be surrounded as well as outnumbered. Our scurvy scoundrels are no match for their trained troops.'

St Leger grimaced and his fingers ran nervously over his sword's scabbard.

'The General is a merciful man. He won't send his men to their destruction for no good reason. You're right, Morrison. Any hope of success disappeared with Castagnier. Very well. I'll inform Tate that we'll leave the legion rather than lead our men to certain death.'

SIXTEEN

AMBUSH AT MANOROWEN

Under a dappled sky of mauve and grey which was beginning to deepen into black, Lord Cawdor and almost fifty blue-uniformed cavalry rode towards Manorowen.

Earlier in the afternoon, his forces had joined with Colonel Knox's Fencibles at Trefgarne. Cawdor now commanded a hotch-potch army of Militia, Fencibles and Milford Haven seamen totalling nearly seven hundred men. And behind this strange collection of red, green and blue uniforms, two nine-pounder cannon clanked along in a couple of handcarts.

At first, a heated argument had taken place between the two men as neither was willing to relinquish overall control. Only when Colonel Colby, who commanded the naval volunteers, sided with the older man had Colonel Knox grudgingly agreed to accept Cawdor's leadership.

Tom's heart swelled with pride as the sound of fifes and drums grew louder. His mother and Megan were safe at home after their stroll on Bigney Hill, but his feet had proved too itchy to remain with them. A little guiltily, he had slipped out of the back door and then Fishguard itself. It was only a mile to Manorowen farmhouse where he now awaited the arrival of Cawdor's forces.

Out of the corner of his eye, a sudden strange movement caught Tom's attention. He turned and stared into the gloaming. Ghostly silhouettes of armed soldiers were sneaking across the farmyard towards the summerhouse. It was too gloomy to see the colour of their uniforms, but British soldiers would have no need to act so surreptitiously. They must be Frenchies!

The blood drained from Tom's face and he shrank back into the safety of some gorse bushes. Slender boughs scratched at his ears and neck while he considered the situation. Unarmed and alone, he knew it would be folly to do anything other than warn Lord Cawdor of the French ambush. In his glittering uniform and riding a magnificent charger, the Commanding Officer would make an easy target.

'Make haste,' he told himself. 'Lord Cawdor's life may depend upon it!'

Furtively, he slipped into the dusk and then began to race along the turnpike road towards the advancing British army. Through the gathering darkness he flew, as if a demon was on his tail.

When he came within a hundred paces of the column, he yelled, 'There are Frenchies ahead!' His lungs felt on fire so he paused to cool them with some deep draughts of damp air. Then he repeated, 'There are Frenchies at Manorowen farmhouse!'

Suddenly, a mounted officer loomed over him

and demanded, 'Are you sure, lad?' The first Baron Cawdor could hardly credit that the enemy was so close.

'Yes, sir. Quite sure!'

'How many of 'em, do you think?'

'I saw less than a dozen, sir.'

Lord Cawdor turned in his saddle and said to the nearest young officer, 'It's probably a scouting party. Take the cavalry and flush 'em out. The time for talk is over. Now the hunt's afoot!'

With that, the Castlemartin Yeomanry moved forward at a canter, leaving a trail of mud in their wake. No sooner had the night swallowed them than the unmistakable report of pistol and musket-fire, and some shouting, echoed in Tom's ears. The sounds were frightening, yet exhilarating at the same time. But the exchange was brief. The youngster was not alone in praying that the Frenchies were already dead.

When the snorting, sweating horses returned, the exultant officer panted, 'The French have fled, my lord! It seems there were only a handful of them.'

'Any casulaties?' Cawdor asked.

'None, sir.'

This news pleased Tom, but Lord Cawdor's face remained grave. He stared at Colonels Colby and Knox who had been summoned for a parley.

'Gentlemen, this means there are French troops on the loose less than a mile from Fishguard. Lord Milford's orders are clear. At all costs, we must prevent the enemy from breaking out of their position on the Pencaer peninsula. If the only way to do so is to attack tonight, so be it.'

'But it is very dark, my lord,' Colonel Knox objected. 'And the only roads are narrow lanes and cart-tracks. At most, we could advance three or four abreast.'

'You really must try to be more positive, Knox,' Cawdor replied, with more than a trace of venom in his voice. 'Such pessimism does not become a King's officer. The French are in a panic and retreating already. We will advance. Without delay.'

The younger man suppressed the desire to reply in kind. Relations between the two were evil enough already. Knox bit his tongue and contented himself with saying, 'Then I shall give the order, sir.'

Standing in the shadows, Tom heard every word of this bitter exchange. He took a step or two forward and declared, 'My lord, please let me join you! I know how to use a musket and, if you're going to attack the Frenchies tonight, you'll need every volunteer you can muster!'

Lord Cawdor laughed. He looked into Tom's bright eyes and asked, 'What's your name, lad? And how old are you?'

'Tom Phillips, sir. I'm sixteen.'

'Well, Master Phillips, you're a brave fellow and no mistake. You've done your family proud by saving us from an ambush, so the least I can do is grant such a heartfelt request. Report to Lieutenant Hopkins, our artillery officer, at the rear of the column. It will be the devil of a job manhandling our cannon along rough cart-tracks at this time of day. He'll be glad of your assistance, I'm sure.'

Then Cawdor wheeled his horse, dug his spurs into its flanks and rode into the night.

Though Tom was dismayed at being offered such a menial, unheroic task, he dutifully reported to a stocky, blue-jowled officer who ordered him to get behind a farmcart and push. Then he pointed to one of the cannon above them and added, 'If we have to fire that beast, boy, keep well out of her way! A nine-pounder roars and flames like an angry dragon. And when she rears up and flies backwards, she slays anyone who gets in her way. So treat her with respect.

'War isn't a game, lad,' he continued. 'It's blood and pain and shattered bodies. Understand?'

This weird, but vivid, warning impressed Tom. 'Yes, sir!' he barked. He was now aware that being posted to the rear did not mean out of harm's way.

By the time they had hauled the brace of cannon within firing distance of the enemy, Tom's fair hair was matted to his skull, his hands were a bloody mess and every muscle in his body seemed to be burning.

SEVENTEEN

ST LEGER STANDS FIRM

'Mary, Mother of God, the night is black as pitch so grant me sharp eyes,' prayed Barry St Leger. 'And let this arrogant English general – whoever he is – get his just reward for risking his men's lives so recklessly. Amen.'

The young officer drew his sword and spoke to Captain Brémond, who often acted as his interpreter. They listened as the sound of beating drums and marching feet drew nearer. 'That's a fearsome noise to hear when yez can see nothing. Tell the men not to be afraid. Tell them that the British must be led by madmen to attack us at night. Tell them they'll be safe as long as they keep their wits about them.'

Brémond barked out a French version of the Irishman's address to the anxious soldiers. Though there were low mutterings, they realised that it was too late now to do anything other than follow orders.

'My grenadiers will advance into the fields where they must lie flat on their stomachs until I give the order to form ranks. Then they'll fire by platoon. In their dark uniforms, the British won't see them until it's too late. They'll march headlong into our trap! No matter how many troops they have, no matter how well-trained they are, we shall blow them to smithereens before they can return fire!

'Then we'll withdraw and rejoin yez here, Brémond. God willing, I shall have some good news for General Tate at last.'

A look of horror crossed Thomas Nesbitt's lined face. The retired officer, who had been placed in charge of the team of British scouts by Colonel Knox the previous day, could hardly believe his tired eyes as he watched Lord Cawdor's force advance onto the Pencaer peninsula. It was a foolhardy decision. Hundreds of French grenadiers lay in wait and most of the British soldiers would be unable to return fire or charge without endangering their own comrades. If the enemy kept their heads, the British would certainly be slaughtered. His stomach churned as he envisaged the spectacle of a bloody rout.

'What's Knox playing at?' he muttered. 'I know he's young but it's not his way to be so hot-headed. Jones, you've the swiftest legs. Report to Colonel Knox as fast as you can. Tell him that he's about to be ambushed and will suffer grievous losses unless he withdraws immediately!'

The unexpected arrival of a scout bearing such desperate news caused Knox considerable consternation. He was well aware that, in some quarters, he was judged too concerned with his own safety and too ready to order retreat. But this advice was unequivocal. There was nothing for it but to urge, in the strongest terms, that the attack be aborted.

To his surprise, Lord Cawdor did not demur. 'Sound the recall,' he ordered. 'We'll do as Nesbitt suggests. There are regular troops on the way. Tonight, we'll rest in Fishguard. Tomorrow, we shall put the French to the sword!'

When Tom found himself shoving a cannon in the opposite direction from the invaders, he was not best pleased. 'We'd have driven those damn Frenchies into the sea by now!' he declared, but Lieutenant Hopkins just shook his head knowingly.

By the time Lord Cawdor's troops trudged into Fishguard, they were exhausted. Most had walked upwards of fourteen miles that day. The cold streets were lit with flaring torches held aloft by the cheering townsfolk. The sharp-witted soldiers swiftly sought lodging in local houses, but the slower souls had to sleep in the streets or in the surrounding fields.

The officers, whose elaborate uniforms drew admiring gasps from the onlookers, headed for The Royal Oak where Major Meredith had been kicking his heels all afternoon. Tom knew the Major was expecting to be involved in military matters at the inn, so he made his way there rather than for home where his mother and Megan were anxiously awaiting his return.

Tom was friendly with Morgan Williams, a pot-boy who worked at the inn, so he went directly to the kitchen-door at the rear where he was challenged as to his business by a burly sentry.

He replied, 'I'm Thomas Phillips, manservant to Major Meredith,' and was granted entry.

The smell of roasting beef accompanied him up the staircase. He entered a large, over-heated room where several officers, most of whom he did not recognise, were engaged in earnest conversation.

'Tom!' Major Meredith exclaimed. 'What brings you here?'

Dressed in puritanical black, the Major stood out like a sore thumb amidst the colourful array. But, unlike his peers, he had promised his Dissenter wife, on her death-bed, that he would never wear his uniform again. And Owen Meredith was not a man to break his word.

The youngster thought it best not to mention his part in the skirmish at Manorowen farmhouse nor his brief involvement with the British artillery. Instead, he simply said, 'Lord Cawdor and Colonels Colby and Knox will be here at any moment, sir. And I thought I might be of service.'

For some reason, which he could not fathom, this caused several of the officers to grin and one of them – a Colonel James of the Cardigan Militia, Tom later discovered – burst out laughing and roared, 'Well, lad, you can run downstairs and get me some bread and pickle! I'm famished and will surely faint if I don't get some victuals inside me soon!'

But before Tom could undertake this errand, Lord Cawdor swept into the room.

'Gentlemen, we have serious issues to discuss,' he declared, in an imperious voice of command.

With that, Major Meredith motioned his head for Tom to leave. His servant did so reluctantly, closing the door on a Council of War.

EIGHTEEN

TATE'S TERMS

'I've fought many battles and often been up to my ankles in blood, but my heart has never failed me before,' General Tate confessed. His voice was icy.

'Hundreds of infantry, and cavalry, you say?'

'Yes, sir,' St Leger answered. 'Six or seven hundred, at least. When they advanced towards us a short time ago, we managed one volley before they withdrew without returning fire. Captain Morrison has also received reports that there are more than a hundred troopers on Bigney Hill.

'Commodore Castagnier's departure this afternoon has caused panic amongst the men. They feel they've been left here to die and many of them are refusing to obey orders. We're on the brink of mutiny! And we are surrounded by superior British forces. It is our considered opinion, sir, that we should surrender.'

Tate's grey face contorted with disappointment. 'What you say is true. Our troops are in disarray. But I don't understand why the Welsh peasants haven't rallied to our cause. Can't they see that we're risking our lives to give them a better future?

'Before I make a final decision, I want to speak to the Quartermaster. If we've sufficient transport, perhaps we can yet break out of here without suffering grievous losses.'

But the Quartermaster's report only confirmed what most of the officers already knew. There were no horses, no wagons, no cattle and provisions were dangerously low. The local livestock had been wiped out and the men were still ravenous.

The issue was settled.

'Bring me paper and a pen,' Tate ordered. Without a further word, he dipped a quill into an ink-pot and began to write his terms for surrender in a shaking hand.

It read:

Sir,

The circumstances under which the body of the French troops under my command were landed at this place renders it unnecessary to attempt any military operations, as they would tend only to bloodshed and pillage. The officers of the whole corps therefore intimated their desire of entering into a negotiation upon principles of humanity for a surrender. If you are influenced by similar considerations you may signify the same by the bearer, and, in the mean time, hostilities shall cease.

Health and Respect,

Tate, Chef de Brigade.

General Tate took up the paper and crossed the room, his long shadow cast by the flickering candles. He read it again and closed his eyes. The shame of defeat was pricking them with tears. He sealed the finished letter and thrust it at his second-in-command. 'Tell their Commanding Officer that my terms are for the immediate return of all our troops to France. Take l'Hanard with you as he speaks English so well.'

Le Brun paled visibly as he handled the document. 'Yes, sir,' he mumbled. 'I shall deliver it forthwith.'

It broke St Leger's heart to see the old man in such an abject state. The General's long blue coat and white waistcoat suddenly seemed grubby and dishevelled. He looked frail and frightened. But, as an American citizen, he faced imprisonment, at worst. The Irish officers, as rebels against King George, might be tried for treason. Lieutenant St Leger's forehead beaded in sweat as he contemplated his own execution.

At nine o'clock that night, Jacques Phillipe Le Brun and Francois l'Hanard reached the outskirts of Fishguard in order to sue for peace.

NINETEEN

LORD CAWDOR'S RETORT

Protected by a flag of truce, the French officers were met by Thomas Williams who guided them to The Royal Oak.

Bemused and uncertain, the two men were jostled and jeered by a howling, fist-shaking mob but they reached the inn unharmed. At once, Colonel Knox ordered them to surrender their weapons. Then he escorted them inside to meet the Commanding Officer.

When Lord Cawdor read Tate's letter and heard l'Hanard's explanation of its meaning, he realised that he was now in total control of events.

'General Tate's terms are quite unacceptable,' he declared. 'The suggestion that His Majesty's Government pay to transport French troops to Brest is absurd. I have a superior force, both in quality and numbers...'

'We have twenty thousand men under arms!' Knox interrupted intemperately.

Cawdor glowered at the young officer. It was too ridiculous a claim to be taken seriously so he chose to ignore it. He continued, 'General Tate must surrender unconditionally. Nothing less will suffice. He must agree to this by ten o'clock tomorrow morning. Otherwise, I shall attack!'

Le Brun stared at all the British officers in their array of splendid uniforms and realised that the invasion was over. It had lasted just thirty hours.

His thoughts were interrupted by Lord Cawdor informing him that he and l'Hanard would be kept under lock and key. Major Ackland would take his demand for outright surrender to the enemy headquarters.

Cawdor paused to draw breath and then continued, 'Meredith, as you seem the most suitably attired for the part, would you be so good as to undertake the role of secretary? I shall dictate my reply, and you can put it down for me. Your penmanship is bound to be better than mine.'

'Of course, my lord,' Major Meredith replied. He went to the doorway and called for the necessary writing materials. Tom was the first to react to the request and soon appeared with quill, ink and paper in hand.

'Good heavens, it's our will-o'-the-wisp again!' exclaimed Lord Cawdor. 'What on earth are you doing here, lad? I thought I'd assigned you to artillery duties.'

Embarrassment at this revelation caused Tom's face to turn the colour of a ripe plum. He could feel his Master's astonished gaze boring into him, but he did not dare return it.

Fixing his eyes upon Lord Cawdor, he stammered,

'Bu... but, I did follow your orders, sir! I helped pull a nine-pounder to Trefwrgy and back. It was only when I was dismissed for the night that I made my way here. I'm Major Meredith's manservant, my lord.'

'Are you, indeed? Then you're a fortunate man, Meredith. You've a brave, hard-working lad there. I should be more than content to have him in my employ at Stackpole Court.

'But enough of this idle chatter. We have an important document to compose.'

When completed, the letter read:

Fishguard, Feb 23rd 1797.

Sir, The superiority of the force under my command, which is hourly increasing, must prevent my treating upon any terms short of your surrendering your whole force prisoners of war. I enter fully into your wish of preventing an unnecessary effusion of blood, which your speedy surrender can alone prevent, and which will entitle you to that consideration it is ever the wish of British troops to show an enemy whose numbers are inferior. My Major will deliver you this letter and I shall expect your determination by ten o'clock, by your officer, whom I have furnished with an escort, that will conduct him to me without molestation.

I am etc. Cawdor.

Cawdor handed the historic paper to Major Ackland and said, 'Deliver this to General Tate at the French headquarters in Trehowel. Make it clear to him that his only choice is unconditional surrender. No other terms are acceptable. A troop of cavalry will escort you.'

'Aye, sir,' snapped Ackland, accompanied by a salute. Then he spun on his heel and was gone.

'Well, gentlemen, before we turn our attention to the pressing matter of roast beef,' laughed the Commanding Officer, 'raise your glasses and let us toast the King.'

As one, a roomful of officers stood and roared, 'The King!'

When news spread that the French officers had come in search of peace and Ackland's mission was to demand outright surrender, there was rejoicing in the streets of Fishguard. Ale and wine flowed, songs were sung and heartfelt prayers of thanksgiving were offered.

But Major Meredith's thoughts were elsewhere. He was anxious to discover what Tom had been up to in the hours since he had last laid eyes upon him. He was also concerned about Mistress Phillips who would surely be fretting about the whereabouts of her wayward son.

'We shall repair to your home at once. There, you can recount your adventures and, no doubt, make profuse apologies for your disobedience,' the Major warned.

Tom argued feebly, 'Though I didn't seek permission to go to Manorowen, sir, I was never denied it. And, as you ordered, I haven't laid a finger on any musket.'

Such sophistry cut no ice with the Major. And, for

a few minutes, Tom's mother was more vexed with her son than she had ever been. But when he told of his advance onto the Pencaer peninsula in the darkness, Mistress Phillips put her head in her hands and began to sob. She loved her only child dearly, and now she realised that she could have lost him.

'Lord Cawdor shouldn't have allowed a mere boy to take the field!' she cried. 'If you'd been killed, what would I have done? Left alone in a world at war.'

The taste of triumph had turned to ashes on Tom's tongue, but he began to appreciate the depths of a mother's love for the first time in his short life. Guilt at the awful anguish he had caused turned his eyes as watery as October sunlight. He looked imploringly at his mother.

There was a light touch on his arm. He turned and saw Megan beside him. 'For pity's sake, Tom, go to your mother and tell her how sorry you are,' she urged. 'This should be a time of celebration!'

'Well said, my dear,' added her father, who was so relieved his daughter had broken the unbearable tension that he gave out a full-bellied laugh.

Tom did not need a second bidding to take his mistress's advice. He rushed across the room and threw his arms around his mother's neck. Hugs, kisses and apologies flowed like wine at a wedding. 'I'm so sorry, Mam! I've been thoughtless and selfish, but I'll be a more dutiful son in future.'

Clouded by tears of joy, Tom peered at Megan and wondered what it would be like to walk from church with such an intelligent and beautiful woman on his arm. What a lovely bride she would make! He could hear the minister saying, 'I now pronounce you man and wife. You may kiss...' It would be a happiness beyond his powers of imagining.

TWENTY

SURRENDER

When Major Ackland strode into the unkempt farmhouse at Trehowel with the demand for unconditional surrender, Tate refused to agree to it.

'I'll consider the matter overnight,' he vowed. 'And I will send an officer with my reply in the morning.'

This unexpected response caused Lord Cawdor a sleepless night, but the French commander was merely delaying the inevitable. He had no other option open to him. Shortly after dawn, he summoned Lieutenant Faucon and handed him a terse note agreeing to the British terms.

By nine o'clock, on 24 February, 1797, the fresh-faced officer stood outside The Royal Oak inn. When he was summoned into Lord Cawdor's presence, Faucon – along with Le Brun and l'Hanard – signed the surrender document to which General Tate added his name later that day. It was a humiliating experience for all four men. As Tate put his quill to paper, he still could not understand how his mission had ended so disastrously.

'Surrender your arms at low tide on Goodwick Sands,' Cawdor ordered. 'My men will supervise the affair and then will escort your troops to

Haverfordwest where they will be interned as prisoners-of-war. I give you my word that all will be treated with respect and due decency.'

At midday, with the Fishguard Fencibles and Cardigan Militia lining the beach at Goodwick and more troops stationed on Bigney and Windy Hills, the French had still not made an appearance. Hundreds of excited locals, who had come to witness the historic occasion, began to murmur amongst themselves. Had Cawdor been duped? Were they all now caught up in a cunning French conspiracy?

Lord Cawdor glanced at Captain Edwardes and swore. 'Damn their Frog eyes! Ride over to Trehowel with a couple of cavalrymen and find out what the hell Tate is up to! His men should've been here hours ago. My patience is running low. Tell him they've got until two o'clock. Then, by God, we attack!'

When Captain Edwardes pulled up his horse outside Trehowel, he was astonished to see that many of its window-frames had been torn out and used for firewood. But his presence and Cawdor's ultimatum prompted his French counterparts to marshall their troops and begin the long march from Pencaer into captivity.

By two o'clock, to the onminous beat of bass drums, the first Black Legionnaires reached Goodwick Sands and began to place their largely unused weapons into piles. Raucous shouts and cheers rang out from the crowd of Welsh onlookers until, around four o'clock, the last enemy soldiers surrendered their muskets. Stripped of their arms and dignity, the scowling Frenchmen trudged off the beach towards Haverfordwest gaol.

Head bowed and dressed in a shabby, ill-fitting uniform, James Bowen did his best to be inconspicuous. He stared resolutely at the wet sand in an attempt to avoid eye-contact with any of the local folk. If the cry of 'Traitor!' went up, he knew he was done for.

Only eagle-eyed Tom Phillips spotted him. For a moment, he was tempted to reveal the blackguard's presence in the enemy ranks but, for some strange reason, he could not bring himself to do so. Bowen faced a grim future in a British prison and possibly the hangman's rope. What could be gained by witnessing a howling mob execute summary "justice" by tearing him limb from limb?

No, Tom was in too good a humour to do such a thing. In fact, he was grinning like a feeble-minded inmate of bedlam. Megan, as fresh and pretty as an April primrose, stood beside him. All he could think about was what a lovely bride she would make.

At the rear of the French column, he also noticed a small number of junior officers who had been detailed to keep a wary eye out for stragglers and a rump of recalcitrant republicans who hated the very idea of surrendering to His Britannic Majesty's forces. Amongst them was Lieutenant St Leger. Momentarily, Tom's eyes met Barry's, and the coincidence changed their lives for ever.

The broad-shouldered Irishman strode across the wet sand and nodded amiably to Tom, but he addressed Megan, 'To be sure, I never expected to see those sparkling eyes again! I've always said that luck is worth more than gold. It seems mine is running out, but I'll pray that God will continue to bless yez, miss.'

At the handsome officer's compliment, Megan's eyes seemed to melt and her mouth widened into a soft smile. 'Thank you, sir,' she replied. 'For being kind to us the night before last, you deserve a little luck yourself, I think.'

St Leger bowed his head and said, 'It was the least I could do, miss. Reluctantly, I must leave yez all now as a prison cell awaits me.'

The Lieutenant extended his arm and Megan did likewise, expecting him to shake her hand, but St Leger bowed again and kissed it instead. It was a gesture which sealed his place in Megan's heart. As he walked away, a tear or two tumbled down her astonished face.

Major Meredith was slack-jawed at what he had just witnessed and Tom could not contain his indignation. 'An officer who can't control his men shouldn't have such a high opinion of himself!' he sneered. 'He allowed his troops to get drunk whilst he skulked in the dark like a schoolboy.'

'Come, come, Tom,' Megan retorted, 'Lieutenant St Leger was genuinely concerned for our safety, and you know it!'

Tom scowled at her loyal defence of the enemy. 'He was the best of a villainous bunch, I suppose,' he admitted grudgingly.

Meanwhile, at Trehowel farmhouse, an exhausted and dispirited General Tate was still waiting for British soldiers to arrive and take him into custody. When he heard the sound of footsteps creak on the floorboards, he stood up and made his way to the door, where he was surprised to discover a civilian inspecting the damage done to the premises.

Both men were nonplussed. Then Tate unbuckled his sword and, in a dignified fashion, handed it to the stranger, with the frank admission that his courage had deserted him as soon as he had set foot on British soil.

Thus the Fates decreed that John Mortimer, the Welsh farmer whose home had been ransacked and used as the enemy's headquarters, and not Lord Cawdor, took a part in the final act of surrender.

TWENTY ONE

MEGAN'S MISSION

Pentower's front door was ajar. Major Meredith pushed it open and was followed inside by his daughter and servants. It was obvious that the house had been looted in their absence. Anything capable of being carried – even the brass candlesticks – had been stolen. The kitchen had been ransacked and the larder and wine-cellar were bare.

When the Major climbed the stairs and witnessed the damage which Bowen had inflicted upon his portrait, a stabbing pain shot through his middle-aged heart forcing him to grab the bannister for support. But the painting of his beloved wife was unharmed, and he knew of an artist in St. David's who could replace his own. Soon they would be side-by-side again. This thought comforted him and released the vice which had gripped his chest.

The servants busied themselves and Pentower was swiftly restored to something like normality. Some broken chairs had to be removed for repair, but the house had suffered few of the indignities inflicted upon Trehowel.

Later on, Major Meredith adjourned to the round tower and began to tug at a stone which formed part of its battlements. It resisted him for a while, which was a relief because, behind this ancient rock, lay a leather pouch bulging with a hundred gold guineas. Only he and his daughter knew of its location. The bag was still in its place. Their secret was safe. The Major smiled contentedly. Other than Megan's strange reaction to the enemy officer's attention yesterday, life already seemed back on an even keel. But as soon as he returned to the farmhouse, Megan asked, 'What will become of St Leger, father?'

'Most of the Frenchmen are being held in the castle gaol and various churches in Haverfordwest, but the talk is that the enemy officers will be taken to London for trial,' he replied. 'General Tate will probably be imprisoned, but I fear for the Irishman. He could be tried for treason which, to judge from your kind words about him, would be a pity.'

A look of utter despair clouded Megan's wan face. 'Surely they couldn't hang such a gallant gentleman!' she protested.

'The Home Secretary, His Grace, the Duke of Portland, will make that decision, my dear. It's not for the likes of us to do so.'

'But it would be a dreadful injustice to execute him! Will you write and beg for clemency, father?' she pleaded. 'Were it not for the Lieutenant, I shouldn't be alive!'

Major Meredith was shocked by her urgent tone. 'I think, my dear, that you owe your life to Tom Phillips and Jemima Nicholas, and not that Paddy!' he said sharply. 'He did no more to protect you than any gentleman should've done. Nothing is to be gained from my penning such a letter. Rebels against the King must be be punished. It's time to put this experience behind us.'

Megan realised that to argue further was futile. Her father was determined on the matter. But someone had to save St Leger. The Irishman was charming, and had the face and bearing of an Adonis. If nobody else would undertake the mission, then *she* would!

Saint David's day came and went. Tom was helping the cook, Mrs Thomas, in the kitchen when the Master hurried into the hot room. He looked flustered and sounded breathless.

'Have either of you seen Megan?' he enquired.

'No, sir,' they replied in unison, glancing quizzically at each other.

'Where on earth can she have gone? She's not slept in her bed and some of her clothes are missing.'

What the Major did not add was that the pouch of gold guineas had also disappeared like a phantom in the night. The dreadful notion dawned that his daughter – still several months short of her eighteenth birthday – had stolen his savings and gone on a madcap search for the silver-tongued prisoner.

'Tell Dai to harness the coach and horses, Tom. We've a long journey ahead. I'll pack a bag. And, Mrs Thomas, some victuals and cider to take with us, if you will.'

'Where are we going, sir?' an excited Tom asked.

'Oh, you misunderstand me, lad. I should be glad of your company, but Dai and I will have to manage. You must stay here and take care of Pentower. Almost daily, there are reports of more French landings on the Welsh coast. Whether they're true or not, I need to know the house is in safe hands. I've great faith in you, Tom. Now don't let me down.'

An hour later, Major Meredith's carriage pulled away in a cloud of dust. Tom watched until it disappeared from view.

At that very moment, General Tate was unceremoniously bundled into a coach in Carmarthen. He, Le Brun and the three Irish officers were on their way to face justice in London.

Lord Cawdor, who was tired and irritable after a fire in the town during the night, travelled in a carriage with Le Brun who, though smelling like a pig in his unwashed uniform, was of noble birth. Tate and Tyrrell were escorted by Joseph Adams in a second carriage. The short procession of coaches ended with one carrying Lord Edward Somerset who accompanied Morrison and St Leger.

Their route to the capital lay through Llandeilo, Brecon, Gloucester and Oxford. Several times, the coaches were attacked by angry mobs intent upon overturning them. On such occasions, William Tate – now an embarrassment to the National Cockade of Republican France which was still pinned to his chest – cowered in terror.

Eventually, the prisoners reached London unscathed and were examined in the Admiralty boardroom by members of the Privy Council. St Leger glanced anxiously around the magnificent room with its classic columns, ornately carved ceiling, high windows and walls covered in rolled charts. He and his fellow Irishmen insisted that they had never known their destination was Britain, while General Tate begged not to be returned to America. It was decided that these men posed little threat to the nation's safety, and the Duke of Portland ruled that they should be exchanged for British prisoners held in France.

In the weeks which passed for this judgement to be reached, Major Meredith scoured London for his daughter. He searched high, amongst magistrates and ministers of the crown and cloth, and low, amongst clerks and thieves, but all in vain. His funds were almost spent, and he was not even sure that Megan had made her way to the capital. Had he leapt to a hasty conclusion? As Dai optimistically reasoned, it was quite possible that his remorseful child was already back home in Pentower. After weeks of fruitless searching, the Major took the practical decision to abandon his quest.

What he did not know was that, more than once, he had missed meeting his daughter by a matter of moments. Day after day, in all weathers, Miss Meredith stood outside the Admiralty building with her paid companion, Ann Roberts, a skittish girl whose acquaintance she had made in the milliner's in Haverfordwest. Megan awaited news of the fate of her Irish hero with increasing foreboding.

One bright, breezy morning, she flashed her pertest smile at a boyish-looking officer and asked, 'Sir, do you know what is to become of that villain

Tate and the rest of his crew?'

The young man returned her smile and replied, 'They're all to be sent to a prison ship in Portsmouth harbour, I believe. May I be of any further assistance, miss?' he asked.

Megan shook her head. 'No, no, sir!' she replied, dashing his hopes. There was a distant gleam in her eyes as she thought of another handsome officer.

She turned to Ann and said, 'We must take a coach to Portsmouth. Today.'

TWENTY TWO

THE DUEL

Stems of sunlight poked through the lancet windows of Picton Castle. A musty, leathery smell pervaded the library where its owner was lounging on a chaise-longue.

'Ah, my dear fellow, come in,' said Lord Milford, when the door opened. 'You look well. Command obviously suits you.'

Lord Cawdor strode across the room and, without waiting for any invitation, sat down on a gilt-framed chair. Milford stood, handed his visitor a letter and said, 'I've been awaiting a chance to show you this message. It's from the King himself, congratulating you and Colonels Knox and Colby upon your brave and determined leadership in the recent crisis. He particularly praises you – in the most effusive fashion – for your exemplary courage and skill.'

As Cawdor read the letter, he shook his head. 'Colonel Knox does not merit such flattering words, my lord. That young man is a coward.'

Lord Milford's jaw dropped at his companion's astounding reply. 'Come now, John,' he said, 'King George makes it clear that he's quite content with the part Knox and his Fencibles played in the affair.'

'Then the King is mistaken, sir!' Cawdor retorted. 'Knox thought it prudent to provide for his own safety rather than that of the townsfolk of Fishguard. Of that, there can be no doubt. His order to spike the cannon at the Fort was a dereliction of duty, and the gunners were brave to ignore such an unworthy instruction.'

'But Colonel Knox feared the French might turn those guns upon the town!' Milford protested. 'A mistake it may have been, but it was an understandable decision.'

'No, sir, it was a damned disgrace!' Cawdor snapped. 'His officers and men were appalled at their commander's behaviour throughout. On their behalf, I feel duty bound to insist that Colonel Knox be required to resign his commission forthwith.'

'Oh, my dear fellow, surely that is going too far! It's easy to be wise after the event. Knox may have made some errors of judgement, but a charge of cowardice isn't warranted.'

Lord Cawdor ran his fingers through his hair in exasperation. 'I've spoken to most of the officers who took part in the recent action, my lord, and we are agreed that, if Knox does not resign his commission, we shall tender ours. As you know, I'm not a man to make idle threats. You must choose, sir. Either Knox is finished, or I am!'

The ashen-faced Lord Lieutenant replied tetchily, 'If you feel so strongly on the matter, then I shall ask Colonel Knox for his resignation. But I don't appreciate being brow-beaten into making such a request, sir. Indeed, I do not!'

Within days, a Major Williams arrived at Minwere Lodge, the Knox family home. He explained that he had been sent by General Rooke to investigate serious charges which had been levelled against the Colonel's conduct during the recent invasion.

'I have already spoken to the Governor of Fishguard Fort, the artillerymen there and several officers who served under your command, sir, and I'm afraid there seems to be substance to their complaints,' the Major reported bluntly.

Thomas Knox's volcanic temper was on the point of erupting. 'Good God, man, the Lord Lieutenant has told me that the King himself expressed satisfaction with my part in the defence of the county! Surely His Majesty's opinion counts for more than that of common gunners?'

'Oh, indeed, it does, sir,' Major Williams agreed. 'And the Duke of York has written to General Rooke making it plain that there is no question of a Court Martial being held into your conduct. Royal approval is not in question.

'The fact remains that most of those who hold commissions in this county refuse to accept your leadership. In dangerous times, the Lord Lieutenant cannot be placed in such a dire predicament.'

'Can't you see that Cawdor is intent on dragging my reputation through the mud?' Knox thundered. 'I must see the letter so that I can answer its malicious charges!'

'That is your prerogative, sir,' Major Williams replied. 'But, for the sake of all concerned, I would urge you to bow to the inevitable.'

A week later, Lord Cawdor rubbed salt into Knox's wounded pride by refusing to divulge the contents of the letter of complaint to General Rooke, but he wrote that 'your inexperience and ignorance of your duty, joined to want of judgement' were its cause.

This hurtful reply rustled in Knox's shaking hands. Outranked and outnumbered, he was overwhelmed by a sense of despair. His eyes began to brim with tears of humiliation, something which had not happened since he was a boy. If he could lay his hands on Cawdor's throat, he would throttle the blackguard.

'That's it!' he cried. 'I'll challenge the devil to a duel! Then we shall see which of us is a coward. If it's the last thing I do, I'll send that evil swine to Hades!'

Thomas Knox was already awake when the sun edged over the horizon on 24 May, 1797. He had never felt less like facing the dawn of a new day. The morning was sunny and warm, fit for a picnic, but he and Lord Cawdor had agreed to meet at noon for a duel – to the death.

Though he had delayed the moment of departure as long as possible, he now found himself riding slowly towards the turnpike road between Williamstown and the ferry on the north side of the Cleddau river which they had chosen as the lonely location.

Cawdor would be accompanied by his good friend, Joseph Adams, who had agreed to act as his second. Colonel Daniel Vaughan had volunteered to be his own assistant.

'Duelling is a barbaric business, Tom. Nothing is to be gained from it,' Colonel Vaughan argued, in a last attempt to persuade the young man to retract his challenge. 'It's not too late to see sense.'

Knox thumped the pommel of his saddle and snorted, 'And lose what little that remains of my reputation? No, sir! Colonel Colby has informed me that he would not sign Cawdor's letter because he knows I've always acted with integrity. Nevertheless, I have been obliged to resign my commission. I must make Cawdor eat his vile words, sir. My honour demands it.'

A tight-lipped Lord Cawdor also suggested that the young man had redeemed himself by being present for the duel and that there was no need for bloodshed. But, though his palms were oily and the perspiration prickled on his forehead, Knox was determined not to retreat again.

'There can be no going back now, sir. Once the pistols are primed, I shall have the satisfaction of restoring the Knox name, which you have laboured so cruelly to destroy.'

Cawdor scowled and snapped, 'Then choose your weapon and let's be done with it.'

The tangles of tension in Knox's neck and gut twisted tighter and tighter as he waited, in the soporific sunshine, for the seconds to prepare the weapons. Then the duellists, both dressed in white shirts and linen breeches, stood back-to-back. As Colonel Vaughan counted loudly to ten, they strode apart. At a distance of only twenty paces, each man turned and stared into the eyes of his sworn enemy.

But the sun was shining with a dreadful brilliance into Knox's face. He blinked, only to find false images on his eyes. He could not see! His head began to swirl and he felt faint, but he knew he must not falter. His hands were trembling so badly that he had to use both hands to raise the pistol. He tried to pull the trigger, but his fingers refused to obey orders. Though soaked in sweat, he froze.

Cawdor pointed his pistol to the ground. 'Will you put the gun down, sir?' he called out. His opponent's face was as white as a death-mask.

An uneasy silence descended upon the scene. Even the birds seemed to stop singing.

Without saying a word, Thomas Knox took a step backwards, clicked the hammer and put the pistol onto the grass.

'Gentlemen,' shouted Colonel Vaughan, 'the matter is concluded.'

TWENTY THREE

ESCAPE FROM PORTCHESTER CASTLE

'This hell-hole is intolerable,' muttered General Tate. 'The stench and the heat are such that it won't be long now, my boy, before I give up the ghost.'

The interior of the prison ship, The Royal Oak, was so fetid and humid that Barry St Leger was in the habit of walking about stripped to his tight waist. He saw to it that Tate had use of a hammock, whilst he slept on the bare deckboards, and tried his best to care for the old man. St Leger rarely moaned about the appalling indignities, preferring instead to plot and scheme to escape the wretched place.

'Yez must ask for parole again, sir,' he suggested, in an effort to raise the General's spirits. 'In exchange for yer liberty, offer to negotiate the freedom of a senior English officer...'

Before he could conclude his practical advice, a

guard entered and informed them that they would shortly be transferred to Portchester Castle, a massive fortress outside Portsmouth.

'Thank God!' Tate declared. 'I've heard that conditions in the gaol are much better than here. At the least, we should have a modicum of privacy.'

Life proved more bearable ashore. There were fewer rats and the prisoners were allowed to sit around talking and gambling in relative comfort. But Barry St Leger did not idle his time away. Using crude tools fashioned from animal bones, he organised the digging of a tunnel underneath the stout castle walls. Removing the surplus soil, and the indifference of most of his French allies, made progress painfully slow so that, by the time summer's heat had given way to autumn's rain, the tunnel was only a few yards long.

When one of the guards approached him, in a strangely furtive fashion, on an early October day, St Leger assumed that his tunnel had been discovered. Glumly, he awaited the bad news. But he was taken aback when the pock-faced private whispered, 'I've a message for you, Paddy. From a young Welsh lady. Seems very taken with you, she does. Prepared to pay me well to – shall we say – facilitate your early exit from this 'ere place.'

'What do yez mean exactly?' St Leger demanded, intrigued but suspicious. 'What's this lady's name?'

'No details, Paddy. That'd be silly. Next Sunday, when you're off to Chapel for one of your unholy masses, I'll see to it that the side-door is unlocked. As you're an officer, it should be easy enough for you to slip out unnoticed. Only you mind! I'm takin' a fearful risk, as it is. But the lady in question will make my old age comfortable, if I gets you away, so I'll do my bit. Just make sure you keeps your gob shut an' do yours! Right?'

A bemused St Leger said nothing, but nodded his agreement.

The guard continued, 'On the Lord's Day, the warders can be a little lax, especially when their palms are greased. Do what I say an', in a few days, you'll be in the arms of your lovely lass again.'

As he was still an innocent with women, St Leger had no inkling of the identity of his mystery benefactress. But the guard's urgent tone and demeanour were convincing and, if the door proved to be unlocked, the Irishman meant to take advantage of it.

What concerned him was the General's depression and failing health. Could the frail warrior survive without him? Then came another shaft of unexpected news: his superior officer would soon be returned to France in an exchange deal for British officers. At last, there was a smile on Tate's grizzled face. Now there was nothing to deter St Leger from attempting to escape.

Sunday dawned dull and dreary but the Lieutenant was as excited as a child on Christmas morning. When the Chapel side-door yielded to his touch, exactly as foretold, he almost uttered an involuntary yelp of delight. With difficulty, he controlled his emotions and slipped silently into the Chapel's shadows where the unnamed guard was waiting. He held out a ragged uniform into which St Leger changed and they made their way to the castle's rear gate. Knowing glances were exchanged with the doorman to assure him that he would be well-rewarded for letting them through. Not a word was spoken as the thinly-disguised prisoner was ushered into the street.

The guard smiled with relief as the gate shut. Then he pointed his finger towards freedom.

'That way, Paddy. She's waiting for you. Be off now. An' make sure I never lays eyes on you again!'

St Leger did not need a second bidding. He could see two females in the distance so he hurried towards them. When he was close enough to recognise Megan's pretty face and shy smile, he went gratifyingly red and returned it warmly. Had he been even nearer, she would have seen that his hands were trembling. Since he had first laid eyes on her on the clifftop near Carreg Wastad, there had been a special place in his heart for Miss Megan Meredith. And now this lovely young woman, clad in a scarlet cloak and bonnet, was responsible for his escape from prison!

As Megan curtsied, she felt a surge of joy so intense it astonished her. She thought, 'I don't know why, but I love you, and will love you till the day I die.'

St Leger bowed, grinning like a giddy drunkard.

He had never been happier in his life. Miss Meredith lit a fire in him that brought roses into his cheeks.

He took her hands in his and unleashed all of his Irish charm. 'Miss Meredith, I'll forever be indebted to yez for what you've done this day. I am so happy that 'tis yerself who has come to my rescue. There's no-one in the whole wide world to whom I'd rather owe my liberty!'

'You had no-one else, Lieutenant. And the honour is quite mine,' Megan replied.

She felt his muscular arms encircle her waist. They smiled, and then they kissed. ·

TWENTY FOUR

A LETTER FROM AMERICA

The wars with France dragged on until the battle of Waterloo in 1815. Shortly after the Duke of Wellington's momentous victory over Napoleon, a sealed letter arrived at Pentower. It came from the United States of America, and was addressed to Mister Thomas Phillips. It read:

> *St-Leger's Farm,*
> *Charleston,*
> *South Carolina.*
> *All Saints' Day.*

My dear Tom,

As you were always so loyal to my beloved father, I am writing this letter in the hope that you are still employed at Pentower and may, some day soon, read its contents.

The years have rolled away and Christmas-tide is approaching once more, but I could not bear another to pass without wishing you and your mother the compliments of the Holy Season.

Perhaps I should be sending this to my father. I suppose writing to you is a cowardly way of doing things, but I treated him so shamefully by stealing his life-savings and eloping with my darling, Barry, that I cannot bring myself to do so. Please tell him that I love him and pray for his good health and happiness every night before I go to sleep. One day, I hope to be forgiven for my selfish ways.

We were little more than children when we last met, in the spring of 1797, which is when I went to London, and thence to Portsmouth, in search of the man I loved. I used all of my father's money to purchase my darling's freedom from prison. I was so overwhelmed by my emotions that I did not hesitate to marry him, in a Roman church, a few weeks later.

Thereafter, we made our way across the Atlantic Ocean to South Carolina, where my new husband's uncle owned a farm. We have lived here peacefully ever since and have been blessed with four healthy children. Our eldest son we called Thomas – in your honour. This was Barry's suggestion for, as he often says, you were like a guardian-angel to me and we owe our happiness in life to you. I hope God has been good and also granted you children. I know you must be a most loving and devoted parent.

The sixtieth anniversary of my father's birth is

approaching and I fear that he will never hold his grandchildren in his arms. This thought makes me weep so that I cannot stem the flood of tears. My dear husband is so concerned for my well-being that he has insisted I write to you in the hope that you will persuade my father to travel to our home near Charleston to visit us. You must accompany him, of course, as it is an arduous journey for a man of advancing years. But now that Britain's wars with France and America are over, it is a safe enough voyage.

I cannot wait to kiss my dear father's forehead again and to get on my knees to plead for his forgiveness. Do this one last kindness for me, Tom, I beg you!

I remain your humble and devoted servant,

Megan

The letter threw Tom into a state of emotional turmoil. Of course, he was gratified to discover that Megan was alive and well – indeed, flourishing – but he was utterly downcast to realise that it would no longer be possible to dream of the woman he loved returning to Pentower.

He was now thirty-five years of age and had spurned several chances of marriage because he had always believed that Megan loved *him*. What a fool he had been!

He crumpled the letter and threw it on the floor. His life lay shattered there with it. The blow had come so unexpectedly, like a thunderbolt, that he could not gather his thoughts. The room seemed to swim about him.

Tom sat in a trance, staring through a leaded window at the thick flakes of snow which were falling from a slate-grey sky and silently softening the winter landscape. His thoughts drifted back to that February night when he and Megan, their hands entwined, had stared in horror at the French ships in the bay. How black they had looked!

He remembered the stomach-turning terror they had felt when they were captured and gazed into Jim Bowen's leering, lustful face. He remembered stealing poor Gaspard's musket and the lucky shot in the dark which had saved Megan's life. He remembered Jemima Nicholas parading her Frog captives through the streets at the end of a pitchfork. He remembered the look of sheer disbelief on Lord Cawdor's face when he was warned about the French ambush at Manorowen farmhouse, and how clever Lieutenant Hopkins had convinced a naïve boy to steer clear of a cannon's recoil. He remembered the stuffy room in The Royal Oak filled with uniformed officers holding their Council of War, and the roars of rejoicing which resounded around Fishguard when the two blindfolded French officers had arrived seeking surrender. He remembered clever St Leger, dark-eyed and dashing in his blue uniform, striding across the wet sands at Goodwick to speak to Megan.

But until this fateful moment, he had not appreciated the true significance of their short conversation. Though he was still grateful for such stirring memories, he had never felt so abject and lonely.

He crossed the room to poke at some logs in the grate. Then he picked up the letter, smoothed its creases and began reading it again.

As he did so, Major Meredith, now silver-haired but still powerful-looking, entered the room and brushed some melting snowflakes from his shoulders. He noticed his servant's pallid face and asked, 'What ails you, Tom? You look as if you've seen a ghost.'

The younger man grinned ruefully. 'In a way, I have.' He paused, then handed the letter to the Major. 'I think you should read this, sir. It's from Megan.'

'Megan!' the Master exclaimed as a sharp, but fleeting, pain shot through his chest. 'Thank the Lord she's still alive! But why has it taken so long for her to contact us?'

'Everything will become clear, if you read it,' Tom advised.

As Major Meredith did as he was bidden, tears trickled down the lines etched into his face by years of worry about his lost daughter. His old knees began to shake so he sank into a chair and sobbed, 'Of course I forgive her! My dear child is happily married. How could I be sad about that? And I'm a grandfather too!'

The Major lifted his eyes to the portrait of his

late wife which was hanging on the wall above. She seemed to be looking down on them. 'No man ever had a better wife, Tom. She was even more beautiful in life than on that canvas, and she had the sweetest nature. Even though he's a Papist, she would have approved of St Leger because she believed in the power of love... I'm sure she's smiling at us right now.'

'But it's the other picture that speaks to me,' Tom said, and he fixed his gaze upon the Major's likeness. The strong jawline suggested a strength of will which could be severe, but the artist had also captured tenderness in those deep, blue eyes. 'The one which talks of loyalty and duty. We must go to America, sir, so that you can tell Megan you love and forgive her. She must know that her health and happiness are all that really matter.'

The ageing man watched Tom closely as he was speaking. He opened his mouth as if he wanted to say something but could not. Then he looked at the picture of his wife again, laughed aloud and declared, 'Yes, we'll go to South Carolina! I must see my darling daughter again. I shall kiss her lovely face, and I'll take my grandchildren in my arms. We'll make that journey, Tom. By God, we will!'

He paused to catch his breath, then continued, 'When Megan left, I thought my life was finished. I didn't want to go on. There seemed nothing left for me in this world. Without you, I couldn't have borne her loss.

'You speak of loyalty and duty so passionately that it makes me realise how few fathers have been blessed with sons as devoted and caring as you've been to me. One day, you and I will put all this behind us and we'll have to face the future alone. It may take months, even years, but the time will come. We must accept what has happened rather than fill our remaining days with regrets.

'In the New Year, we'll set sail for America but, before we do so, I intend to draft a new will. And, come what may, Tom, *you* will be the next Master of Pentower!'